Climbing the Rainbow

Also by
Joy N. Hulme

Through the Open Door

Climbing the Rainbow

JOY N. HULME

HARPERCOLLINS*PUBLISHERS*

Climbing the Rainbow

Printed in the United States of America. For information address HarperCollins Children's Books, a division of HarperCollins Publishers, 1350 Avenue of the Americas, New York, NY 10019.

www.harperchildrens.com

Library of Congress Cataloging-in-Publication Data

Hulme, Joy N.

Climbing the rainbow / Joy N. Hulme.—1st ed.

p. cm.

Summary: In this sequel to "Through the Open Door," ten-year-old Dora makes a quilt to record her experiences as she finally starts school and her Mormon family's efforts to secure homestead rights for their farm in New Mexico.

ISBN 0-380-81572-9 — ISBN 0-06-054304-3 (lib. bdg.)

[1. Frontier and pioneer life—Fiction. 2. Schools—Fiction. 3. Mormons—Fiction. 4. New Mexico—Fiction.] I. Title.

PZ7.H8845Cl 2004 2003004448

[Fic]—dc21

Typography by Karin Paprocki

1 2 3 4 5 6 7 8 9 10

First Edition

For all the wonderful people
who fill my life with
RAINBOWS

Climbing the Rainbow

1

You'll Start in First

The day I entered the classroom for the very first time, I was floating on a cloud of happiness. I walked to school with Ed, Caroline, and Frank, as I had done many times. Always before, after the teacher came out and rang the bell, I would watch everyone else file into the building. Then I would go home. This time, I looked down to make sure my shoelaces were tied, smoothed my new blue calico dress, took a deep breath, and walked eagerly up the steps and through the open door.

"Good morning, Mr. McLaughlin," I said, pronouncing the words very carefully. "My name is Dora Cookson, and I'm going to be in your class this year."

"Good morning, Dora," he replied warmly. "Please find a seat."

I looked around, but the room was so full of children I could see no empty spaces.

A tall, dark-haired girl smiled at me from the back of the room and pointed to the seat beside her.

"I'm Cora Beth Tracy," she whispered as I sat down. Already I could tell that she was going to be my friend.

"Boys and girls," Mr. McLaughlin announced, "I want you arranged in alphabetical order by grade. The fourth grade students will sit in the back row, the third grade next, then second. First graders belong here." He indicated the front seats with a sideways sweep of his hand. "Now, everyone please stand at the side of the room and move as quickly as you can to the proper place when I call your name."

What was my proper place, I wondered uneasily as Cora Beth moved away from me to the fourth grade row.

Before long, I was the only one left standing.

"You must be Dora Cookson," the teacher said, looking at his list. "Which grade are you in?"

"I'm not sure," I said.

"Not sure?" he asked in a puzzled voice. "Every other girl knows what grade she's in."

"I've never been to school before," I told him.

"Surely you're old enough," he said kindly. "Have you been ill?"

"Not exactly," I told him. It made me uneasy that all the children in the room were listening. I was afraid I might stutter, so I walked over to the teacher, stood on my tiptoes, and whispered in his ear.

"I couldn't talk."

Mr. McLaughlin could tell that I was embarrassed. He leaned down and spoke very quietly.

"You seem to be talking fine right now," he said.

"I had an operation."

"An operation, yes . . ."

"My tongue had to be cut loose where it was tied down."

"I see," he said. "And when was that?"

"Nearly a year ago," I told him. "The day before we left Utah to come to New Mexico."

"And after that, you learned to talk?"

I nodded.

"You learned very well."

"I can read, too," I told him.

"But you've never been to school?"

"No."

"Then you'd better start in first grade," he said, "and we'll see how it goes."

As I took my seat in the front row with all the little kids, I heard plenty of snickering.

"Isn't she older than Ed?" one boy whispered.

"I think she's ten," another replied.

"Must be pretty dumb," a third added.

I am not dumb, I thought, turning to see who said that. It was a big boy with messy, mousey hair sitting in the fourth grade row right next to Cora Beth. *I'll show him,* I decided, *that I am NOT stupid.*

Catching my eye, Cora Beth smiled. She waved her hand a tiny bit as if she were saying, *Have courage.* She tilted her head slightly and looked toward the window. "I'll see you at recess," she mouthed, and I smiled, happy to have something to look forward to.

If I had a new friend, it wouldn't matter so much that Lucy Williamson was in the room next door or that Jenny Lenstrom went to a different school. Lucy and Jenny were my church friends. I saw them every week when we went to Clovis for Sunday School.

I found out right away that a lot of things go on at once in a classroom with four grades. While one group repeated memorized poetry, another one worked out arithmetic problems. Second graders copied spelling words from the blackboard, and we first graders practiced printing our ABC's. After a while, each class activity changed.

It was hard for me to concentrate on first grade things because I wanted to pay attention to everything else. I'd overhear a snatch of something the teacher was talking about to another grade and I couldn't quit listening. My hungry mind was starved. The classroom seemed like a feast of knowledge, laid out on a table, inviting me to gobble it up.

Before I knew it, we were dismissed for recess and I stood outside with Cora Beth.

"Don't pay any attention to Toby Tully," she said, jerking her elbow at the boy who'd called me dumb. "That big bully is always looking for someone smaller to pick on."

"I wish I could sit by you," I said.

"Me, too," she agreed. "How come Mr. McLaughlin put you in first grade?"

"It's a long story," I said.

"Tell me," Cora Beth replied, pointing to a bench where we could sit down.

"This is my first day in school," I began.

"How come?"

"I wasn't allowed to go," I said.

"Why not?"

"I couldn't talk."

"Not at all?" Cora Beth asked.

"A few mumbly sounds," I said, "but no words. Everyone thought I was stupid."

"How awful."

"Yes, it was."

"So what happened? You talk fine now."

"I had a bad earache," I explained, "and had to go to the doctor . . ."

"And?"

"He discovered my tongue was stuck down to the floor of my mouth. It couldn't move up or down like it is supposed to. 'Tongue-tied,' he called it."

"So what did he do?"

"Cut it loose," I said.

"And all of a sudden you could talk?"

"Not all of a sudden. It took a long time. The first thing I did was bite my tongue when it got between my teeth while I was chewing a peppermint stick."

"Ouch!"

"You mean double ouch! It hurt plenty. After that, I had to learn to keep it away from my teeth and to train it to move in all the right directions to make different sounds. It was hard. I ended up imitating my baby brother, who was just learning to talk."

"That was a clever idea," Cora Beth said.

"It worked pretty well," I said. "And my brother Ed helped a lot. We were moving to New Mexico in a covered wagon train with eleven other families. There was no place to be alone to practice."

"But you did it?"

"Yes, and then I started to stutter and Mama was afraid I'd get teased, so she kept me home and taught me to read."

"What happened to the stutter?" Cora Beth asked. "How did you get rid of that?"

"A lot of practicing," I said. "Papa said tongue-twisters with me when we worked in the fields together. It was easier not to stutter when we said the same things at the same time."

"It probably would be," Cora Beth agreed.

"Something else that helps is singing the words. That's how I learned to say 'Mr. McLaughlin.' I pretended the scarecrow was the teacher and sang his name over and over."

"Pretty smart," Cora Beth said.

"I've already read all the first grade books at home," I told her. "And I learned arithmetic by listening to Papa when he helped Ed and Frank with their homework. I love numbers. They just seem to dance in my head and go where they should."

"You should be able to skip some grades and move up."

"You think so?"

"Sure."

"I'd like that," I admitted. "But I'd have to skip three before we could sit together."

"Even then we couldn't sit right next to each other since you are a *C* and I am a *T*," Cora Beth reminded me.

"That's right," I agreed. "I'd be next to Ed."

"At least we'd sit on the same row and be doing the same lessons," Cora Beth said. "I'll help you catch up if you want me to."

"Oh, I *do,*" I said. "I need to. How nice of you to offer."

"That's what friends are for," Cora Beth said.

I knew we could do it. I'd learned to talk, hadn't I? Dreams don't come true because some fairy godmother waves a wand over your head. You make them happen yourself. It takes a lot of hard work, but having a friend to help makes it a lot easier.

Our family was doing the same thing by homesteading a farm. When we left Utah, we expected our new farm to be in Clovis, but it turned out to be closer to Texico, a town that was half in New Mexico and half in Texas. Main Street ran along the state line and divided the two sections. We did our ordinary shopping in Texico and went to church in Clovis.

Our family had five years to prove to the government that we could turn 160 acres of New Mexico land from a weedy cactus patch into neat, productive fields. If we did, we'd own the property. Nearly a year had passed already. Papa had enlarged the one-room shack into a three-room house with a basement. It still wasn't big enough for all nine of us to sleep inside, even with baby Irene in a basket. Ed, George, and I continued to have our beds in the barn loft. We had begged to sleep up there on the mounds of fresh hay when the barn was new. By now, each of us had carved out our own private space.

While we all worked to help Papa break the land, plant a crop, and weed, water, and harvest it, I'd improved my talking so I'd be allowed to go to school. To remember the important things that happened to us, I had embroidered pictures of each event on a sampler. I finished it just before school started. I figured that if my family could do as much as we did that first year in New Mexico, I could easily move up three grades in school, especially with Cora Beth's help.

Ed would help me, too. He was glad I was making new friends at school, but he continued to watch over me like a big brother even though he was a year and a half younger.

One day, a few weeks after school started, when Mr. McLaughlin was teaching the fourth graders about square feet, I got an idea. As with most notions, this one started out small, like a dried-up seed waiting for just the right time to grow.

Although I'd been adding and subtracting numbers in my head for a long time, it seemed strange to see them written down in arithmetic problems on the blackboard. I caught on to square feet right away, though, and figuring out the correct answer to a fourth grade problem tickled me. It felt like my brain was smiling. That's why I was watching the blackboard instead of doing the first grade assignment.

The teacher drew long lines up and down and others across until he had a lot of squares right next to each other. They looked exactly like blocks stitched together to make a quilt.

"Now, students," Mr. McLaughlin instructed, "figure out how many ways you can determine the number of square feet in this diagram while I listen to the first graders read."

I only paid attention to the first part of his sentence.

That's easy, I thought. *Six across and eight up and down. Six times eight is forty-eight.* Next, I began counting the squares. Then I heard my name. Twice. "Dora. DORA COOKSON," Mr. McLaughlin called, "will you *please* quit daydreaming and pay attention to business? In case you haven't noticed, the other first graders have already moved to the recitation bench. It's your turn to read."

I blushed with embarrassment, grabbed my reader, and hurried to the long seat near the teacher's desk. I fumbled to find the right place in my book and began reading.

"'Now who will help me harvest the wheat?' asked the Little Red Hen. 'Not I,' quacked the duck. 'Not I,' honked the goose. 'Not I,' grunted the little fat pig. 'Then I'll do it myself,' said the Little Red Hen. And she did.'"

"Very good, Dora," the teacher said, as if he were surprised. That story was baby stuff! I could have read it with my eyes closed. I knew it by heart long before I could talk. Even if I hadn't, the words were simple. I could read harder books than that!

I wondered what Mr. McLaughlin would say if he knew I'd figured out the fourth grade arithmetic problem in my head. *It's funny,* I thought, *how much can be going on in your brain that nobody else knows about.*

While I walked home after school, the image of the square-foot pattern popped into my head again and I wondered how many blocks it would take to make a quilt. Probably forty-eight, I decided, the same as the pattern on the blackboard. Six long rows with eight blocks each.

By Sunday, the quilt idea had really started to grow. That afternoon I was up in the hayloft, thinking about my goal to catch up to my grade. I wanted to keep a record to help me remember how I did it. Most girls would make entries in a diary, but I was struggling just to learn to write. I was used to keeping track of things by drawing pictures and then sewing them on my sampler. Now I thought about making quilt squares with pictures to keep track of my progress as I moved up from grade to grade. Since Mama had just taught me how to appliqué a design by stitching pieces of material onto a backing, I would use that method as well as some embroidery.

Once the idea sprouted, it grew like a weed, so fast I could hardly keep up. I remembered our family goal—to earn the homestead farm. We still had four years to go to "prove up." The designs could tell an important part of that story, too. Four years. Forty-eight months. Forty-eight quilt blocks. Perfect! I'd make one square each month until the homestead was ours. Two rows across for every year. And six long stripes up and down. The exact number of colors on a rainbow. Red, orange, yellow, green, blue, and violet.

I thought back to the first evening in our homestead house. We had sat cross-legged on the floor, camp-out style, to eat our supper, because we'd left our table and chairs behind in Utah.

As Mama had dished up the bottled peaches, she said, "I have something to show you while you eat your dessert."

She picked up a picture frame that held a black-and-white drawing of a rainbow.

"A rainbow," she told us, "is the symbol of a promise. The promise that God made to Noah after the Flood. I'd like this one to be a symbol to us of the promise that if we work hard for five years, we will have our very own farm."

I noticed that faint pencil lines had been drawn across the rainbow at equal intervals to divide it into five parts. Mama had written a date on each one—1911, 1912, 1913, 1914, 1915. I'd be fourteen years old before the farm was ours.

Mama pointed to the bottom of the arch and followed it up. "It's very steep at first," she said. "It will be hard for us to climb without falling back down. But we'll get stronger and stronger. And once we get to the top, it's downhill all the way." Her finger traced the arch with a quick swoop down the other side.

"It takes both sunshine and rain to make a rainbow," Papa had added. "We'll have some bad times and some good ones. That's the only way we can find out if our backbones are made of starch or jelly. And don't forget that we Cooksons . . ."

All of us knew exactly what Papa was going to say next. We chimed in to help him finish the sentence.

". . . always stick with a job until it's done."

"Without complaining," Papa added.

"Without complaining," we repeated.

Eight-year-old Ed had elbowed me with a nudge that meant *at least not where he can hear it*, and we began to giggle. Caroline, age ten, stared daggers at us to behave. Six-year-old Frank and four-year-old George scraped up the last drops of the peach juice with their spoons, but Howard, who was nearly two, licked the bottom of his bowl.

"Every November twenty-first, the anniversary of the date we filed for the farm, we'll celebrate Homestead Day," Mama continued. "As each year is completed, I will paint the colors on that part of the rainbow." She hung the picture on a nail that had already been hammered into the wall.

Now, nearly a year later, I smiled, remembering that first night in the new house. I thought of the red, orange, yellow, green, blue, and violet bands of color that would soon brighten the first section of Mama's drawing. I could imagine the same sequence of colors on the six stripes of my quilt. A rainbow quilt. How beautiful that would be!

Mama's painting was the reminder of a promise. My quilt would tell how the promise came true. I decided to have one section of twelve blocks finished each year in time for our anniversary celebration. I'd put classroom and farm scenes on the blocks because I'd be keeping track of progress in both places. I imagined the colorful coverlet laid out on a bed! I wanted to tell Mama all about it, and I flew down the loft ladder and across the yard to look for her.

George and Howard were outside with a pan of

soapsuds, blowing bubbles through some empty thread spools. The fragile balls gleamed with the same rainbow colors I was planning. I felt like one of those floating spheres, all lighthearted and glowing, as I ran toward the house.

Then I thought of something that popped the bubble just as fast as if it had bumped into a cactus thorn.

Where would I get the material to make the quilt? I knew there weren't enough plain-colored scraps in the ragbag. And I knew we didn't have enough money to buy new pieces of cloth for the blocks. We were still climbing up the steep part of the rainbow, and pennies were scarce.

I sank down on the porch step, feeling my chin drop with disappointment. I couldn't share my idea with Mama now. She'd only feel bad. I made up my mind that I wouldn't tell her about it at all.

In a moment, though, she came out the door and sat beside me. Neither of us said anything for a long time. Finally she broke the silence.

"What's the matter, Dora?" she wanted to know.

"Nothing," I lied.

"Oh, come now, your face is as long as a cucumber and your smile is turned upside down. Don't tell me nothing is wrong."

"I don't want to talk about it."

"That's all right. You don't have to."

We sat quietly side by side, and she put her arm across my shoulders. I blinked to keep the tears from spilling out.

It was no use. First one fell and then another, and before I knew it, they were pouring down my cheeks.

"Oh, Mama," I wailed, "I had such a good idea, but . . ." The words gushed out until I'd told her all about it.

She nodded her head. "You are quite right. A rainbow quilt is a wonderful idea." She smiled at the thought. Then her face became serious. "But there are no pieces big enough in the scrap bag. And there isn't enough money to buy new material."

All of a sudden her eyes twinkled a little. "But don't forget there's more than one way to skin a cat. We'll just have to put our thinking caps on and see what we can figure out." Mama squeezed my sagging shoulders again, and I started to feel better.

After dinner she asked Caroline to tend Irene while I helped with the dishes.

"I'll wash, Dora," Mama said, "if you'll wipe."

"Okay," I agreed, and picked up one of the bleached flour sacks we used as dish towels. I noticed that a bunch of faded flowers was embroidered in one corner. "Did you make this?" I asked.

"Oh, yes," Mama said. "Long, long ago. I had a whole set when I got married. All bright and new. One for each day of the week. They lasted quite a while, but that's the only one left."

Then I smiled—suddenly I knew that other way to skin the cat!

2

Eager to Start

Mama's embroidered dish towel had given me the idea to use flour sacks for my quilt blocks! Besides the stack Mama had already bleached and hemmed, she had a whole pile of extras. First I would need to unravel the stitching down one side and across the bottom that made each one into a bag. Then the big pieces of heavy muslin could be washed and bleached in the sun. I folded the dish towel I was holding in half and then in half again. Each bag could make four blocks. I would only need a dozen for my quilt, two for each color.

"What happened to my dish wiper?" Mama asked, looking around. "Oh, I see, she's a million miles away, daydreaming about something."

"Umhmm," I agreed.

"Want to tell me what it is?"

I held up the folded dish towel. "Flour sack quilt blocks," I said.

"Good idea! I knew you'd think of something."

"Can we dye them the right colors?" I asked, unfolding the towel and reaching for a plate to wipe.

"Of course," she said, scrubbing at a dirty pan.

"Does dye cost very much?"

"No. It's cheap. I already have red, yellow, and blue. And we can easily mix orange and green. We'd better buy some violet, though. It's always a muddy color when you try to make it with red and blue."

"Can we do them all at the same time?" I asked. "So they'll be sure to match?"

I remembered that some of the watermelon wedges around the edge of my sampler were a different shade of pink because I'd run out of thread and the new skein wasn't quite the same color I'd used to begin with. Even though I knew real melons were different shades, too, the unmatched look on the sampler still bothered me.

"Of course," she agreed. "If you unravel the stitching tonight, I'll wash and bleach the sacks while you're at school tomorrow. I'll give you a dime. You can get the purple dye at Younger's store on your way home."

I was so excited about the quilt blocks, I couldn't wait for tomorrow to come.

❀

Mama had worried that I might be disappointed in school. Several times before the term began she said, "I surely hope that anticipation doesn't exceed realization."

Finally I asked, "What does that mean?"

"It means," she explained, "that I hope you're not expecting too much. You've made up such a rosy picture about school, I don't see how you can like it as much as you think you will."

"Yes, I will!" I insisted.

"Don't be too sure, miss," she said. "Many's the person who got what he wished for and then wished he hadn't."

She needn't have worried. School and I were made for each other.

The two classrooms were separated by a plain wooden wall that was really a huge door that dropped down from the ceiling like the cover on a rolltop desk. Last year all eight grades met in the big room. This year, there were enough students for two teachers. The door was lowered to divide the space in half.

"It sounded like a thunderstorm when they did it," Caroline had told me. "I could hear the rumbling all the way across the street at Younger's. The crash scared me so much I almost dropped the eggs that Mama had sent to pay for the sugar."

Mr. McLaughlin had been hired to teach the lower

four grades in the east room, and the principal was in charge of the upper four in the west. His name, Mr. Stern, suited him fine. My sister was in his sixth grade class.

"He's a cracker," Caroline said.

"Huh?" I questioned.

"He's a cracker," she repeated.

"What's that?" I wanted to know.

"He cracks the whip, cracks knuckles, and cracks heads."

"What do you mean?"

"He runs his class like a lion tamer," she explained. "He snaps out orders like he's lashing a whip. He slaps your knuckles with a ruler if you don't know the answer, and if you talk to your neighbor, he bangs both of your heads together. *Crack. Crack. Crack.*"

"How awful," I said.

"But there are two things you can be sure he'll never crack," she assured me.

"What?" I asked.

"A smile," she said, "and a joke."

After that, I never dared to stick my nose into Mr. Stern's room for fear I'd get cracked like Humpty-Dumpty. I almost changed my mind about wanting to catch up to my class. If I did, the cracker would be my teacher next year.

I was glad I was in Mr. McLaughlin's class. He smiled

a lot—and even cracked a joke now and then.

I couldn't explain how excited it made me to learn something that I didn't know before. It was like discovering a furry nest of wriggling new kittens, watching a chick peck its way out of a shell, or looking at a finished piece of embroidery where I'd made all the stitches perfectly even. I loved the feeling. Nothing was more important to me than finally being in the classroom. What picture would I put on my first quilt block? Would it be the teacher? Arithmetic problems? My new friend, Cora Beth? I wondered which as I waved good-bye to her after school and went across the road to buy the purple dye at Younger's store.

Mama was ready to start coloring the flour sacks as soon as I got home.

"They need to be wet first or they might come out blotchy," she said, and sent me to fill the dishpan with water.

Starting with yellow, the lightest shade, she mixed the powdered dye carefully into a big pot of hot water and added a little bit of clear vinegar.

"What's that for?" I asked.

"To set the color so it won't wash out," she explained. Stirring with a wooden spoon, she boiled the first two flour sacks until she was satisfied with the shade. Then she lifted those into a pan of cold water for me to rinse, wring, and hang on the clothesline while she mixed the next color.

Before long, my bright rainbow pieces were drying in the breeze—red, orange, yellow, green, blue, and violet. They were so beautiful that the sight almost took my breath away. Even the boys noticed.

"What are the flags for?" Frank asked.

"A surprise," I told him. I wanted to have at least one block done to show to the family when I explained my plan at our Homestead Day celebration in November.

As much as I loved school, I hated being teased by the bigger boys. Toby Tully, the bully who had called me dumb on the first day of school, was the worst. "Dumb Dora, dumb Dora, count on your thumb, Dora," he taunted.

"He doesn't have any room to talk," Cora Beth told me, speaking loudly enough for him to hear. "He's the one who does arithmetic on his fingers. And talk about dumb! Tobias is repeating fourth grade *again*." She lowered her voice to a whisper. "He hates to be called by his real name."

Toby walked away in a huff, but I was still angry about being called dumb. I would show the big bully I was not stupid. I'd catch right up to the grade he was in and pass him! In the meantime, I'd figure out a way to stop his teasing once and for all.

Every day I took a reading book home to study. It

was the same one that Mama had borrowed to teach me to read, and I knew most of the words already. I practiced *Henny Penny, The House That Jack Built, The Timid Hare*, and all the other stories until I could read the book from cover to cover without making any mistakes.

The effort paid off. Within two weeks, I was reading with the second graders. The words were harder, but after I was able to sound out the title of the story, *Epamanondas*, I knew I'd be okay.

That same day Mr. McLaughlin decided to promote me officially.

"Everyone on the second row shift over one seat to make room for Dora to sit next to her brother Frank," he instructed.

Maybe my first quilt block would show our desks side by side.

When I told Papa what had happened, he smiled. "So they moved you *back* to move you *up*, eh?" he said. "That sounds contrary to reason. Are you sure it's an improvement?" He tousled my hair in a way that let me know he was only teasing. He was really as proud as punch.

The main problem with being in second grade was learning to write in cursive. That was difficult. The teacher called Cora Beth up to the blackboard to demonstrate how it should be done. She wrote like a dream—every letter even and all of them perfectly spaced.

Fourscore and seven years ago our fathers brought forth . . .

We were supposed to practice rows and rows of handwriting exercises on lined paper—up and down straight lines all slanting at the same angle and flawless circles swooping evenly around and around and around.

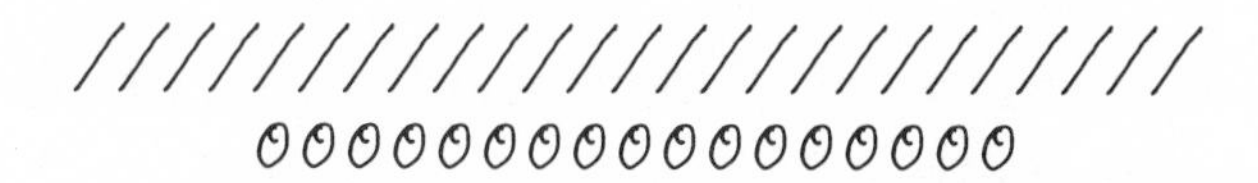

"You need to get a rhythm to your writing," Mr. McLaughlin explained. "Use your whole arm," he instructed. "Let it *flow* from the shoulder."

Cora Beth showed us how. I couldn't do it. I was used to holding a pencil tightly between my fingers and drawing precise little details of a pattern I was going to sew. I wanted to outline the circles one at a time, carefully, so they'd be perfect. I didn't know how to whirl them around with my whole arm the way I was supposed to. I wrote with stiff, jerky movements, and my words came out scribbly and hard to read.

Toby Tully noticed when he passed my desk on the way to the recitation bench. "Don't you *know*," he whispered, "it needs to *flow*?"

"TOBIAS TULLY IS A BULLY," I printed on a separate page large enough for him to see on the way back to his desk.

Maybe my written words were hard to read, but they were always spelled correctly. Once I saw the letters arranged in the right order, I never forgot what they looked like.

As far as I was concerned, though, *writing* spelling words was one thing, and spelling them *out loud* was another. The first was easy, the second hard. I decided that must be because I couldn't visualize what a spoken word looked like. It had to be written down for me to be able to tell if it was right or wrong.

Every month we had a practice spell-off, preparing for the big spelling bee in the spring. I was often the first one to miss a word and be sent to my seat. I soon noticed that the worst spellers in the class were the best writers. I mentioned that to Caroline one day as we walked home from school.

"No wonder," she said. "They get the most practice. Don't they have to write every word they miss on a spelling test at least ten times?"

"Sometimes twenty," I told her.

"Well," she said, "that ought to improve their penmanship."

"It should," I agreed. I never missed the words on a test, but I decided to practice writing them anyway for the sake of my penmanship.

"If you think writing is hard," Caroline said, "just wait till you get to history. That's just a boring bunch of names and dates. And they all have to be memorized. But you won't have to worry about that until fifth grade."

She was wrong on both counts.

I was just getting a good start in second grade when Mr. McLaughlin seemed to disappear into thin air. On Friday he was at school, and on Monday morning he was gone.

The principal met our class at the door to tell us that our teacher's father had died up north in Colfax County and he'd gone home for the funeral. Mr. Stern introduced us to Miss Foster, who would substitute until Mr. McLaughlin returned. She had shiny blond hair and sky-blue eyes and didn't look much older than some of the eighth graders. Miss Foster had what Mama called a passion for history. Evidently she was too new to know that it wasn't supposed to be taught until fifth grade.

She started right in the first day. "Truth is stranger than fiction," she announced. "Just to prove it, we will have real stories, not made-up ones, the last few minutes of the day. Today I'll tell you about Cleopatra." She wrote the name on the blackboard.

"Just imagine . . ." she began in a deep-toned, velvety

voice. She paused long enough for all of us to turn our eyes in her direction. "Imagine that you are the young, beautiful, and brilliant queen of Egypt, Cleopatra."

The rich, exciting sound of Miss Foster's voice when she said "Cleopatra" made me feel like a queen already.

"Your father's will has specified that you are to share the throne with your ten-year-old brother."

I imagined that the second grade seats Frank and I sat in were the twin thrones of Egypt.

"But your brother's guardians want all the power for themselves," Miss Foster continued, "so they drive you, Cleopatra, out of the capital city, Alexandria. They take control of the country in his name . . ."

Miss Foster quickly drew some lines on the board that looked like a tree trunk with a lot of branches fanning out from the top. "Here's the mighty Nile River," she explained, "and here"—she connected the tips of the river branches with another line—"is the Mediterranean Sea coast."

She put an *X* at the farthest left-hand end and labeled it "Alexandria."

"You are over here in Pelusium," she continued, making another *X* on the right side of the map, "trying to figure out how you're going to get the throne back. You know that Julius Caesar, the powerful Roman emperor, is visiting in Alexandria. You are confident that you can persuade him to help you, if you can only get the chance to talk to him. But you know that your enemies will be watching for you. What would you do?"

"Sneak back," Ed blurted out.

"Exactly," Miss Foster agreed, smiling at Ed. "Fearful for your life, in a small boat with very few attendants, you sail in secret along the seacoast until you near Alexandria."

Miss Foster traced the wiggly in-and-out route with her pointer.

"Now the problem is how to get into the city to see Caesar without being recognized and captured. What would you do, Toby?"

"I dunno," he said. "I wouldn't be Cleopatra in the first place. I'd be Caesar."

"Good point," Miss Foster said. "Well, what happened is this: Cleopatra had her servant roll her up in a rug, wrap and tie it like a bale of ordinary merchandise. He carried her over his shoulder past the enemy guards. Can you imagine the smothery feeling? What if you couldn't breathe? What if the carpet dust made you sneeze?"

Just the thought caused my nose to tickle.

"What if the servant dropped you?"

Miss Foster looked toward the back row. "Now, Toby, it's your turn. How would *you*, Caesar, feel when the rug was unrolled at your feet and the most beautiful, bewitching, and important lady in all of Egypt stepped out?" Toby answered by blushing as red as a beet. That minute, just like a light turning on in my brain, I knew how to stop his teasing.

"And girls," Miss Foster continued, "do you suppose that Cleopatra worried that her hair might be messed up or her dress crumpled? If she did, it was an unnecessary concern. Caesar was delighted with what he saw. And then, in her most beguiling voice, Cleopatra asked a favor."

I knew exactly what that "beguiling" voice sounded like. Miss Foster was using it to tell the story. She looked at the clock on the wall. All eyes followed hers. It was time for school to be dismissed.

"What do you think happened next?" Miss Foster asked. "Did Caesar help Cleopatra regain the throne? What did her enemies do? How did her brother act? We'll talk more about history tomorrow."

3

The Small Matter of the Rat

We never did find out what happened to Cleopatra, her brother, or Julius Caesar. Instead, Miss Foster began another real-life story about Hannibal, an African general who crossed the steep and narrow mountain passes of the Pyrenees with elephants. I imagined what it would be like if the huge beasts tried to struggle up the steepest part of the Rocky Mountains back in Utah.

In the days that followed, Miss Foster teased us with other short tidbits from history. When she told real tales about real people, I pretended to be Helen of Troy, Joan of Arc, and Florence Nightingale.

The teacher never mentioned dates, and she always stopped just before she finished a story to ask us, "What do you think happened next?" She never told us the end of the episode. Instead, she said, "Mr. Stern will want to teach you about that. In due time he'll answer all your questions about history."

"Due time" meant, of course, after we were promoted into his class. I decided that history would be one good reason to be in the cracker's room.

I took the second grade reader home every night now, and read it out loud to Mama while she darned socks in the lamplight after the supper dishes were done and the younger children were in bed. She helped me learn how to sound out the words I didn't know. Reading went faster and faster the more I did it. I was trying hard to get as far as possible before Mr. McLaughlin came back. Maybe he would move me into the third grade row if I could read well enough. He hadn't found out yet that I could do all the arithmetic in my head.

I didn't want to think about penmanship. If I formed my letters slowly and carefully, Miss Foster said they looked cramped. If I tried to write fast enough to keep up with my thoughts, even I couldn't read the result.

One day, Miss Foster announced that she had a letter to read to us. It was from Mr. McLaughlin. He'd been gone for two weeks.

Dear Students,

I hope to be back with you soon. Settling an estate takes longer than I thought it would, especially when it's round-up time. We have to ride our horses up in the mountains to find all the cattle and drive them down to the farm before winter comes. In the summer they roam on the range and eat wild grass. This is also the time of year to sell some of them for beef and send them to market. It's a very busy season for ranchers.

I trust that you are giving Miss Foster your undivided attention while I am away and are making good progress in reading, writing, and arithmetic. I would be pleased to have a letter from any or all of you. It would be a good exercise in penmanship, spelling, and composition.

Gertie raised her hand. "What's composition?" she asked.

"Composition," Miss Foster said, "is putting words together to express your thoughts or feelings. Or to tell a story. Tomorrow we will practice by writing letters to Mr. McLaughlin. Did he ever tell you that his father was one of the first Scottish settlers to bring white-faced Hereford cattle to New Mexico?"

Should I stitch Mr. McLaughlin on a quilt block because he was my very first teacher? A red cow with a white face would look nice. Especially on a blue block. Or should I make the square about recess with my new friends?

These days, Cora Beth was teaching me how to run in the "back door" of the jump rope. While Lucy and Gertie turned the rope at an even speed, I could easily enter at the "front door." Just after the rope slapped against the ground, I'd run in and be ready to jump when it came around again. But Cora Beth could go around to the other side and, at just the right moment, run in and jump across the rope as it went *up*. She could do it as easy as pie. I had to count and concentrate and, mostly, miss.

I stood at the side watching the rope and nodding my head to the beat. "Now. Now. Now!" If I hesitated just a second, I'd miss my chance.

Toby Tully didn't make it any easier. He stood on the opposite side and coaxed me to come in at the wrong time. "*Come*, Dora; come, Dora; diddle, diddle, *dumb* Dora," he chanted. His timing had nothing to do with the beat of the rope as it whipped around and around. That really threw me off, and I tripped more than once. I had to do something.

On my next turn, I ran in the front door on the first

turn of the jump rope, chanting,

Tobias Tully thinks he's Caesar,
Falls for Cleo, tries to please 'er.
Cleopatra, Egypt's queen,
Hates Tobias, he's so mean.

I finished by spelling, "T-O-B-I-A-S T-U-L-L-Y I-S A B-U-L-L-Y."

"Tobias is a bully!" the other girls screamed at him, and he took off in a hurry.

Ed, who was watching, pumped his fist in the air as if I'd won a boxing match. His grin told me that he was proud that I could handle Toby by myself.

Getting rid of Toby was one good thing. Even better was the idea that I got from spelling his name to the rhythm of the rope as it slapped against the ground.

"Why don't we practice our spelling while we jump?" I suggested.

"Why not?" Cora Beth said.

"Okay by me," Gertie agreed. Gertie always agreed.

"Not me," Lucy objected. "I'm not going to work during recess."

"Me neither," Mary Jane said. "Let's go play something else."

So they did.

Lucy and Mary Jane were thick as thieves. They

stuck together like glue. Lucy was in my Sunday School class at church, but that didn't mean she was a close school friend. After all, I'd only seen her once a week for a year, and Mary Jane had been with her every school day since first grade. No wonder they were best buddies.

After they left, I spelled the second grade words to the beat of the rope; Gertie, the third grade ones; and Cora Beth, those assigned to the fourth grade. Each of us learned to spell them all. While we were jumping, that is. In the excitement of a spell-down, Gertie became flustered and her mind went blank. I was getting better. But Cora Beth never missed. Never. She was always the one left standing after everyone else made a mistake.

Already I had several good ideas for my first quilt block. Which one should I make? The twin thrones of Egypt? Mr. McLaughlin's cattle? Playing jump-the-rope with my new friends? In the end, I decided to show the kangaroo rat in the teacher's desk drawer.

Everyone liked Miss Foster because she was so young and pretty and nice. The boys loved playing little pranks on her. They often managed to tuck a caterpillar or a stink bug in the handkerchief that she kept folded up in the top drawer of her desk. After being scared into a scream a couple of times when she grabbed the hanky to cover a sneeze, she got into the habit of shaking it out with a careful snap every morning before class began.

One day we were all in our seats waiting for her to wave the hanky and place it on the desk as a signal that class was about to start. When she reached to open the drawer, I thought I saw Frank cover a smile with his hand. Suddenly, a frisky kangaroo rat leaped in front of the teacher's face and hopped across the floor.

Miss Foster screamed and jumped back, upsetting her chair. The tipping chair knocked her feet from under her and she fell over backwards, sprawling on the floor with her skirt and petticoat both flying up at the same time.

The giggles changed to side-splitting laughter, and Frank whispered to me, "I can see her pants!"

"Shut up!" I hissed. "So can everyone else."

Miss Foster had very rosy cheeks when she scrambled to her feet and straightened her dress. She was just picking up the chair when Mr. Stern stormed in. "What on earth is going on in here?" he yelled. "Who is screaming?"

Just then the rat jumped in front of him and he gasped as he leaped out of the way. After he caught his breath, he thundered, "Who brought that beast in here?"

The classroom was as silent as a tomb. Even the rat was afraid to move. Miss Foster quietly opened the outside door, picked up the broom, and nudged the frightened animal until it darted out.

"WHO," Mr. Stern growled, even louder than before, "is responsible for this?"

No one moved. No one spoke. The principal's face was red with rage. The room stayed as quiet as a grave. We could hear a commotion coming through the drop-down door, and Mr. Stern moved to return to his own unruly students.

"We'll settle this after school," he snarled. "If I have to, I'll punish the whole class."

I changed my mind again about catching up to my grade. I didn't *ever* want to be in Mr. Stern's class.

After he left, Miss Foster stood before us. "I trust," she said in a serious voice, "that the offender has learned his lesson and that I do not need to reveal his identity."

It seemed to me that she looked straight at Frank, but then her eyes scanned the room and stopped for a moment on each boy. I couldn't tell if she really knew who did it, but she made each one of them think she did. It was clear to all of us that she didn't intend to tattle to the principal. Mr. Stern would never find out who put the rat in Miss Foster's drawer. In exchange for that favor, we knew she expected better behavior from us in the future.

When the bell rang signaling the end of school, Miss

Foster reminded us to stay in our seats. We sat silently, dreading Mr. Stern's punishment. Would he crack the whip? Crack knuckles? Or crack heads? I wondered.

"WELL?" Mr. Stern thundered, appearing in our doorway.

Miss Foster smiled her sweetest smile. "Mr. Stern," she said in a voice made of honey, "the small matter of the rat has been taken care of."

"And WHO DID IT?" the principal demanded.

"You will be glad to know," Miss Foster continued, "that the culprit has been sufficiently punished. I can assure you that he won't repeat the offense again."

"Well," Mr. Stern said in a more reasonable voice, "he'd better not."

The angry lines on his face seemed smoothed out by Miss Foster's Cleopatra-talking-to-Julius-Caesar voice. I couldn't believe how quickly he'd changed from growling to agreeable—almost as if he were relieved he didn't have to solve the problem. But he wasn't done yet.

"I will not put up with any more pranks," he said. "*No more pranks!* Is that clear?"

After Mr. Stern left the room, our teacher asked, "Did you all understand what the principal said?"

Everyone nodded solemnly. We also understood how she'd saved us from a good cracking. "Then class is dismissed," she said quietly.

For the quilt block, I made the rat with soft gray wool, the desk with brown broadcloth, and sewed it on one of the bright red squares because that was the color of Miss Foster's face when her dress flew up. It was the color of Mr. Stern's face, too.

The next quilt block had an animal on it, as well. A dead one.

4

Please Don't Die

I didn't ever think a pig—especially a dead one—could cause so much trouble.

Raising our own food was a very important part of living on a homestead farm. Even if we didn't have much money, at least we had something to eat. Ever since last spring we'd been fattening a pig for pork.

"It'll be big enough to butcher by fall," Papa had told us.

Papa killed the pig on a Saturday in November while the boys and I watched. A couple of weeks later, Mama and Papa went to Texico to do some shopping. All of us had finished our morning chores, and Howard was helping Caroline make cookies in the house while Irene took a nap. I headed toward the barn loft, where I intended to spend some time with the second grade reader. I changed my mind, though, when I saw Ed, Frank, and George squatted in a huddle deciding what to do with their free time.

"Why don't we play hopscotch?" I suggested, tracing a pattern in the sandy dirt with a stick.

"Naw, that's a sissy game," Ed scoffed.

"Besides, it makes you too hot," Frank said.

"Let's go over to Willie Pearce's and see what he's doing," Ed said.

"Papa said we had to stay home," George reminded him.

"You're right," Frank agreed, probably remembering the time he was punished for disobeying that rule.

Ed stuck a finger into the barrel of pork pickle where some of our fresh meat was curing. He licked the salty juice and coughed like he needed a drink. "Tastes pretty good," he said. "I wonder when the ham'll be ready."

"Long time," I predicted. "Even after it's through soaking it has to be smoked for a while."

"That was some fun," Ed mused, "butchering the pig."

"Yeah," Frank agreed, "watching Papa scrape off all the bristles with a knife, cut it open, pull out all the wiggly, slippery insides, and then hang it upside down to age."

"Sure is funny," Ed said, "all the different ways it

takes to get past the outside of an animal down to the meat. You have to pluck all the feathers off a dead chicken, skin the hairy hide off a beef, and—"

"Scrape the bristles off a hog," Frank finished. "I never figured we'd leave the skin on, but that seems to be the way to do it."

"Why don't we play kill the pig?" George suggested.

"Good idea!" Ed exclaimed. "Let's play kill the pig!"

"Yeah!" Frank shouted.

"You wanna be the hog, George?" Ed asked.

George shook his head.

"Dora?"

"Girls can't be pigs."

"Why not?"

"It's not ladylike."

"Pooh! You're just a scaredy-cat."

"If I'm a cat then I can't be a pig, can I?" I stuck my tongue out at him. "Besides, if you're so brave, why don't you do it yourself?"

"All right," Ed said, "I will! George, go in the house and get some knives." In a few minutes, George came back with three table knives and handed one to me and another to Frank.

"Those aren't even sharp," Ed scoffed.

"They're sharp enough," I insisted.

"We'll need some boiling water," Frank said.

"We can pretend it's boiling," Ed said. "Let's use

the watering trough."

"I'll kill the pig," Frank said. He grabbed Ed by his hair, pulled his head back, and ran the back of the knife blade across his throat.

"Okay," he said, "you're dead."

Ed collapsed to the ground, gave a few violent jerks, and fell back limp, pretending to be lifeless. We carried him to the trough, peeled off his shirt and overalls, dunked him in and out of the water a few times, and laid him dripping on the ground. Then we scraped him with our knives the way we'd seen Papa scrape the scalded hog. Ed was covered with goose bumps from the cold water, but our knives seemed to flatten them out after a while.

He opened his eyes to inspect our work. "I'm still bristly," he said, and we scraped some more. His skin was getting red. Ed looked again. "You missed a few hairs. Better singe them off."

"How?"

"Like Mama does after we pull the feathers off a chicken."

"That might burn you," I worried.

"Not if you're careful. George, bring me a newspaper and a match and I'll show you how."

Ed crunched the paper into a long torch, lit the end, and swept the flame quickly along one arm. We could smell burning hair and see it frizzled crisp against his skin. He rubbed it off.

"See," he said, "clean as a whistle." He did the other arm and stomped on the paper to put out the fire.

"Now you've got to hang me up there where the dogs can't reach," Ed said, pointing to the ridgepole that stuck out from the end of the barn roof.

"How do we do that?" Frank asked.

"Same way as the hog. I'll show you."

Ed undid the rope that let the hoist down and showed us how to tie it to his feet and pull it up again.

Just as Frank secured the rope that left Ed hanging upside down with his feet stretched apart, Caroline called out the back door, "Anyone want some warm cookies?"

"Me!" we all shouted at once, and ran into the house.

"Bring me some," Ed yelled from high in the air.

After a little while I'd had my fill of cookies and remembered Ed. I grabbed a handful for him, ran out of the house, and looked up, ready to toss them to him. His face was fiery red, almost purple. When he saw me, he gasped in a hoarse whisper, "Get me down!"

"Frank!" I screamed, and he came running with George right behind him. I was afraid Caroline might come, too, to see what was going on, but she didn't.

We tried to undo the rope where we'd fastened it around two pegs on the side of the barn, but Ed's weight pulling on the other end held it too tight.

"Hurry up!" he wheezed.

I finally yanked hard enough to give Frank some slack that allowed him to loosen the coils around the pegs. The rope ran fast through our hands and spun around the pulley.

"Slow me down!" Ed screeched as he came hurtling headfirst toward the ground. "DON'T LET GO!"

Just in time, we both tightened our hold on the rope and lifted our feet up to hang on it. Now Frank and I were dangling from one end and Ed, just off the ground, from the other.

"I'm a goner," he whispered.

"Don't let go," I yelled at Frank, "but slide back down the rope. And hurry!"

I followed, and we carefully released enough rope to ease Ed onto the dirt. The blood quickly drained from his face, which became ashy white. His eyes were closed and I couldn't hear him breathing.

"Please don't die, Ed," I begged. "Please."

"Oh, come on, Ed," Frank said in a disgusted tone. "Quit teasing us."

"He's not teasing," I insisted, untying the ropes around Ed's ankles that held him to the hoist. "Get some water."

"What's the matter with Ed?" George wanted to know.

"He'll be all right," I said, partly to calm George,

partly to convince myself. But I prayed silently, *Please, God, don't let him die.*

Frank returned from the trough with his cupped hands full of water and dropped it on Ed's chalky face. Ed gasped and his color started to return.

"Get him a drink," I instructed George, and he ran into the house and came back with a brimming tin cup of water. I held it to Ed's lips, and he sipped some of it. "You nearly killed me," he croaked.

"I didn't mean to!" I apologized.

"Me neither," Frank agreed.

"Whaddaya think Mama and Papa are gonna say?" Ed asked.

"Oh, Ed," I cried, "you're not going to tell Mama and Papa!"

"Why not?" Ed asked, and I could tell by the tone of his voice that he was figuring out how to turn the situation to his advantage. "You know you should be punished."

We couldn't argue with that.

Ed got up and pulled on his shirt and overalls. "Where's my cookies?" he asked. I pointed to the pile where I'd dropped them next to the barn. He walked over, picked up the pieces, brushed off the dirt, and stuffed them into his mouth.

Frank followed him. "Please don't tell," he begged. "I'll do all your chores for a week if you don't."

"I'll help," I offered.

"Me too," George added.

"Pooh," Ed scoffed. "What's a week? You darn near *killed* me!"

"Two weeks?" Frank suggested.

"Not enough," Ed insisted, enjoying his bargaining position.

"Well, a month's the limit," I insisted.

"Okay," Ed conceded. "Thirty days."

"Thirty days?" Frank objected.

"Or I'll tell," Ed reminded him.

"Okay," Frank agreed reluctantly.

"How about you, George?" Ed asked.

"I'll do it," George promised. "And I won't ever, ever play kill the pig again."

"Me neither!" Ed told him.

Ed divided his chores between us, and that night he stood by with his arms folded, supervising while we did them. George was assigned to help Frank dig the potatoes and carrots and store them in the root cellar. I agreed to feed and milk our cow even though I wasn't very good at it. It always took me a long time, and over the next few days, I got further and further behind the extra reading goal I'd set for myself. I expected Mr. McLaughlin to be back anytime, and I wanted to surprise him with my progress.

A cold storm blew down from the north shortly

after Ed's narrow escape, bringing a killing frost with it. Winter had arrived for sure, and my fingers were freezing when I went out to milk the cow. The cold hands on her udder must have bothered Bossy, because she kicked the bucket and sent me sprawling in the mucky gutter of the stable. Ed helped me up, smacked the cow on her behind, and said, "Don't do that to my sister!"

While I cleaned myself off, Ed took the pail and finished filling it so fast that the foam on top was half a bucket thick. Ed didn't expect me to milk for him anymore after that, so I was able to get back to my reading. Frank and George, however, had to pay out their debt for the full month. We were lucky Papa didn't catch Ed bossing the rest of us around to do his chores, but he had been gone a lot lately. He told us he was doing something to help a neighbor but he didn't say what.

I wasn't sure that a five-year-old could keep the secret, but George did. I think he felt guilty that he'd suggested the kill-the-pig game in the first place and didn't want anyone else finding out about it.

On my quilt block, I showed a dead hog hanging from the hoist, not a boy. But every time I looked at it I saw Ed gasping for air. Remembering the color of his face, I used a purple square. That was a scare I could never forget. To myself, I called it the "scare square."

Mama liked to fix special dinners for celebrations. This time of year had plenty of important dates. Our first Homestead Day anniversary was November 21; Thanksgiving, the thirtieth, and Ed's birthday, December 10. After that came Christmas and New Year's.

We had killed the pig in November, partly because the weather was supposed to be cool enough to keep the meat fresh longer, but partly because we had so many holidays coming up.

"I was surely mistaken about the weather," Papa said, wiping the sweat from his forehead shortly after the butchering took place. "I certainly didn't expect this record-breaking hot spell."

"Well, I'm glad we have an icebox so we don't have to depend on the whims of nature," Mama said. "Fresh pork makes meals fit for a king." She was having a good time deciding which kind of meal to have for each special day. She had lots of choices. "Do you want fried pork chops and applesauce?" she'd ask. "Or fresh liver and onions?"

She might serve us heart, brains, tongue, or kidneys. Or cold jellied headcheese seasoned just right and set solid from the gelatin in the broth. We ground some of the meat into sausage and added salt and pepper, sage, and garlic. After Mama fried crisp sausage patties, she made milk gravy in the drippings to pour over mashed potatoes or fresh-baked biscuits.

I always wondered which special day Mama would combine the leftover bits of pork with herbs and cornmeal to make scrapple. That was my favorite.

"Save the spareribs for my birthday!" Ed shouted. We all loved to nibble the crunchy brown meat from the roasted rib bones. Mama cooked them in the oven with baked potatoes, squash, and bread pudding. A whole meal all at once.

"I'll try to save them," Mama replied. "If I keep them right on the block of ice, maybe they'll freeze and then they'll keep longer."

The legs, hocks, and sides of the hog were already soaking in pork pickle, a boiled mixture of salt, honey, saltpeter, and water. After they cured, they would be smoked to make bacon and hams. The fat side pork had been salted down in a barrel in the cellar for use after all the fresh meat was gone.

We munched greedily on the crisp brown cracklins that were left after lard was baked out of the back fat. The snowy-white grease would be used for cooking. The darker fat would be made into soap.

"There's nothing like lard to make a flaky piecrust," Mama insisted. "We'll need it for cakes and cookies, too. But we'll have to get some beef suet for our Christmas pudding!"

Mama didn't have to worry about saving the spareribs for Ed's birthday. During the cold spell, the temperature dropped enough to freeze them naturally when she left them in a covered pan on the back porch.

To celebrate Homestead Day, Mama baked a pork roast in the Dutch oven with browned potatoes, carrots, and apples. Carolyn made a two-egg cake and put one candle in the middle just like it was a birthday. Papa blew out the flame and proudly announced, "Now we have exactly four more years to go before we get the deed to our quarter section of land from the government." Mama pointed to the rainbow on the wall. She had painted the bright colors in the first of the five sections. "We're this far already," she said.

I told everyone about my idea for the rainbow quilt and showed the two squares I'd finished. "I'll do twelve a year," I promised, "until we own the farm."

"That's a good idea," Papa said.

Frank picked up the red square and rubbed a finger across the soft gray shape I'd appliquéd on the block. "This is some kangaroo rat," he said.

"Some hog, too," Ed said, lifting his eyebrows at me, "hanging upside down by its heels."

"Let's eat," I suggested quickly, before any more could be said.

We all took our places at the table, and Papa called on Caroline to say the blessing on the food.

After the meal, I was so full I felt like I'd never need to eat again. But by the next day, I was already hungry and looking forward to a big Thanksgiving Day feast the following week.

That was the same day Cora Beth came to school looking as deflated as a leaky balloon.

5

Now That We're Sisters

When I met Cora Beth outside the classroom door, I knew immediately that something was bothering her. Tears brimmed in her eyes.

"What's wrong?" I asked.

"The new baby was born last night and it's *another* boy." She sobbed.

"Boys aren't so bad," I said, trying to console her, "especially babies."

"But I wanted a sister! Not another brother. That makes *five* now. The only sister I almost had was born dead when I was two years old."

I knew exactly how she felt about wanting a girl after four boys. I remembered how eagerly I'd wished for a baby sister before Irene was born. My wish came true. Cora Beth's didn't.

"I'll be your sister," I volunteered. "It'll be even better to have one your own age than one ten years younger."

Actually, I was six months older than Cora Beth, even though I was much smaller. She seemed to like my idea, though, because she quit crying.

"Then I'll *adopt* you!" she said, and we hugged each other to seal the bargain.

"Now that we're sisters," I began, "that means we *both* have a new baby brother, doesn't it?" I was crazy about new babies. Any kind.

"Sure," Cora Beth answered. "You can be Jimmie Joe's sister, too. He is kinda cute with all that black hair."

"When can I see him?"

"As soon as your mama will let you come over," she told me.

"Today!" I shouted. "Today! Today!"

"O-kay to-day," she agreed, making the words sound like the beginning of a jump rope rhyme.

"I don't even know where you live," I said.

"Straight down the road that goes in front of the school," she said, pointing west. "It's the first house past the third farm on the right."

"My house is the second place in the opposite direction," I said, turning that way to go home.

Mama heartily agreed that a new baby should be

seen as soon as possible. Right after school, she put Caroline in charge at home and walked over to the Tracys' with me. She took a loaf of warm bread and a pan of scrapple for their supper, and I carried a jar of spicy apple butter.

"How much farther is it?" I asked as we passed the school.

"Did you say three homesteads?"

"That's right," I agreed.

"If each farm is half a mile square," she said, "how far is it to go past three?"

"A mile and a half?"

"Right," she agreed. "Just a hop, a skip, and a jump. We'll be there in no time. We ought to invite the Tracys over for Thanksgiving dinner," Mama suggested. "A new mother won't feel like cooking a big meal so soon."

Neither of us had met Mrs. Tracy, but Mama always volunteered to help anyone who might need it.

"I've already asked the Williamsons," Mama reminded me, "because they fixed such a good dinner for us last year. Remember how wonderful that home-cooked meal tasted after traveling nearly two months in a covered wagon?"

"I sure do," I said. "It was delicious."

We started talking about the long trip from Utah to New Mexico, and in a hop, a skip, and a jump we'd passed three farms and were knocking on the Tracys' front door.

Cora Beth introduced us to her mother and showed us the baby. Jimmie Joe was darling, but still a bit wrinkly and red. He looked a lot like Cora Beth.

I told our mothers that Cora Beth and I had adopted each other so she could have a sister.

"How nice," Mrs. Tracy said. "I'll adopt you, too. We need another girl in this family."

"Well, you got a good one," Mama said proudly.

Mrs. Tracy was delighted with Mama's invitation for Thanksgiving dinner. She was happy to be excused from cooking. "But I at least have to bring the sweet potato pie," she insisted. "Mama already sent the pecans from Georgia to trim the top. Cora Beth will help me make it. Do you have enough plates and silverware?"

"Probably not," Mama admitted.

"Then I'll bring some."

There were twenty people for Thanksgiving dinner, plus the new baby. Papa had to put all the leaves in the table and find some boards for benches. The older children took their plates into the front room and sat on the floor.

I hadn't thought about it until I saw them all together, but when Cora Beth and I adopted each other, the new arrangement gave us each *nine* brothers: mine: Ed, Frank, George, and Howard; and hers: Sam Houston, Robert Lee, Peter Paul, Billie Bob, and Jimmie Joe. Just as all the names in the Cookson family went down the alphabet, the Tracy names were always double. Poor Lucy Williamson, who was an only child, was overwhelmed by so many boys. I tried to imagine making that many brothers on a quilt block and decided not to do it.

The minute Cora Beth saw nine-month-old Irene, she fell in love with her. No wonder. Jabbering all the time, nearly ready to take her first step, Irene looked like an angel with curly blond hair and big blue eyes.

"Now I have a baby sister!" Cora Beth exclaimed.

"And an older one, too," I reminded her. "Caroline."

"That's right!" she said. "All of a sudden, my family's a lot bigger."

After the meal was over and the Williamsons left, Cora Beth asked me, "How come you call Lucy's folks Brother and Sister and mine Mr. and Mrs.?"

"Oh, they belong to our church," I explained. "We call everybody Brother and Sister."

"Then Lucy is your sister, too?" I detected a bit of disappointment, almost envy, in her voice.

"I guess so," I said, then hastened to reassure her. "But it's not the same as having an *adopted* sister."

"I'm glad," she said, sounding relieved, and wrapped her arms around me.

Right after Thanksgiving weekend, Mr. Stern came into our room to make an announcement. "Mr. McLaughlin," he said, "cannot get away from his responsibilities at the ranch at this time and will not be back. Miss Foster will continue as your teacher." Everyone clapped because we all liked Miss Foster so much.

"That will do!" Mr. Stern barked. "Such demonstrations are not necessary."

I could tell that Miss Foster appreciated it, though, because after he left she said quietly, "Thank you for your vote of confidence." Her eyes were shiny with unshed tears.

I probably loved Miss Foster as much as anyone. Even so, my stomach gave a little flip-flop. What would happen, now, to my hope of moving ahead to the third grade? Would Miss Foster allow me to advance as easily as Mr. McLaughlin had? I was determined to prove to her that I deserved it.

Once the canning was done and the crops harvested, farms settled down for a rest, and neither Cora Beth nor I had as many chores at home. We spent a lot of time at each other's houses, enjoying Jimmie Joe and

Irene and playing house with our dolls. Mine, named Henrietta, had a stuffed leather body and a china head and hands. Her painted blue eyes stayed open all the time. Rose Marie, Cora Beth's doll, had eyes that closed when she was lying down. We played so much that I got behind on my reading. I mentioned this to Cora Beth because she was as anxious as I was to have me skip some grades.

"Why don't you read out loud to the babies when we play house?" she suggested.

So I did. Irene loved to cuddle up on my lap and listen to *Johnny-Cake, The Wolf and the Seven Little Kids,* and other stories in the second grade reader. Jimmie Joe looked around with big bright eyes, soothed by the sound of my voice. When he yawned at me and went back to sleep, I lowered my voice to a whisper or else made up a tune and softly sang the rest of the words like a lullaby.

Just before school was out for the Christmas holidays, Mr. Stern had some of the eighth grade boys help him roll up the heavy door that divided the two classrooms. He wanted to make a place big enough for our families to attend the Christmas program we'd all been practicing.

Mr. Stern's students had learned to sing in parts, and were going to do the carols and the bell ringing. Our room was supposed to act out the Bible story about the birth of the Christ Child. Cora Beth was picked to be Mary. She had longer hair than anyone else, and when she undid the braids, it fell past her waist in beautiful, silky waves. It was even as black as Mary's must have been. But I think the main reason she was chosen was because she had a new baby brother. Cora Beth was supposed to bring Jimmie Joe to be a real live Baby Jesus.

Toby was perfect as the grumpy innkeeper, and Ed played the part of Joseph. The rest of us were either shepherds or animals or angels. I wasn't surprised at all when Miss Foster asked me to be an angel. Blond, curly-haired girls with dimples never had a chance to be anything else.

My sketches had won the contest for decorating the room, so I stayed after school to help Miss Foster get things ready. What I saw on Mr. Stern's blackboard helped me make up my mind forever about catching up to my class.

I was standing there staring at it when Miss Foster said, "It looks like you'll need to erase the board before you start drawing on it."

But I couldn't. Someone had put words and lines in designs all over the blackboard. Some words were sitting side by side on a line like a shelf in the middle of the air. Some were sliding down slanting lines that connected to others below. Some were separated from their neighbors by short marks like closed doors. The words didn't make sense to me the way they were arranged. I was trying to puzzle them out when Miss Foster turned around from hanging up some tinsel to see how I was getting along with my part of the decorating job.

"Can you figure out all that sentence diagramming?" she asked kindly.

I shook my head. "I've never seen anything like it before," I told her. "What does it mean?"

She picked up Mr. Stern's pointer from the desk and touched the words as she read the sentences the way they should go.

"Why are they done like that?" I asked, pointing to the neat patterns on the board.

"To analyze the parts of speech," she said.

"How does it work?" I wanted to know.

She laughed. "It would take too long to explain now. Wait till you get in Mr. Stern's room and he'll tell you all about it. Now, erase it quickly so you can make your Merry Christmas pictures." I hated to wipe out all those word designs, but finally I did.

While I was drawing the holly and candles and Christmas bells, I thought about the sentence diagrams. Seeing them made me more determined than ever to get promoted into Mr. Stern's room. I'd just have to figure out how to get along with him. Miss Foster had proved that his anger melted away if he was spoken to in a gentle voice. Even if I got cracked a time or two, it would probably be worth it.

While we decorated the room, I told Miss Foster about my idea of catching up to my grade.

"Maybe it's possible," she said. "I've never seen a student who learned any faster than you do. But it's highly unlikely that anyone could do four years' work in one."

"In two years," I said quietly.

"How do you figure that?" she asked.

"One at home," I reminded her. "While I learned to talk. And to read."

"That's true," she agreed. "You are a good reader. And you're already doing fourth grade arithmetic." She'd noticed!

"And spelling," I reminded her.

"Yes . . ."

Miss Foster left the word hanging in the air, as if she were thinking about what to say next. "Yes," she repeated after a while, "I'll bet you could do it. You really should be in a grade with children your own age."

She fastened a paper chain to the door frame. "If you stayed an extra hour after school two or three days a week," she said, "I could help you then. I'm really too busy to do it during school time."

"I will!" I promised. "And I'll study hard at home."

"But," Miss Foster said, "I'd just as soon not make a big to-do about it. I don't want everyone in the room to decide they should go skipping through school. Let's just do it and keep it to ourselves. We'll gradually move ahead but not announce any promotion until the end of the year."

"Yes," I agreed, thinking how nice it would be to surprise everyone. Everyone except Cora Beth. She already knew.

"Especially," Miss Foster went on, "since I can't *guarantee* that you'll skip all the way into fifth grade. I'll just promise to help you get as far as you can."

I grabbed Miss Foster in a tight hug. "Thank you," I whispered, trying to put as much feeling into the words as she did when she told us stories.

"I could take some books home for the holidays," I suggested.

"That's a good idea," she said. "I'll pick some out for you. You're ready for the third grade reader already. But your penmanship needs some work."

"I'll practice," I promised.

"I'm sure you'll need to be able to write neatly in pen and ink before Mr. Stern will allow you to skip into his room."

"Mr. Stern has to allow . . . ?" I asked. I hadn't thought of that.

"Of course, he's the principal."

I'd have to write nicely in pen and ink? With a stiff, scritchy, scratchy pen? And drippy, droppy, blotty ink? I'd *never* be able to do it.

I didn't pay much attention to the Christmas program except to make sure that I walked out with "the multitude of the heavenly host" at the right time and said, "Glory to God in the highest and on earth peace, goodwill to men." The rest of the time I was worrying about writing well enough to skip into fifth grade. After the play was over, the room buzzed with proud parents. Cora Beth looked beautiful as Mary, and Jimmie Joe slept through the whole thing without making a sound.

Christmas was the Monday following the program. There was no money for our family to buy gifts for each other, but we drew names anyway and each of us made something for the one whose name we had chosen. My present was for Caroline. I made her an embroidered pillowcase from a bleached flour sack. I stitched a dress for Cora Beth's doll, Rose Marie, too. My friend didn't know how to sew yet, but I was teaching her.

Like the year before, we found a kosher weed tall enough to decorate for a Christmas tree. The cone-shaped plants grew wild along the fence line and were as stiff and prickly as their tumbleweed cousins. We made paper chains and popcorn strings and looped them in swags.

"They look just like smiles," Papa said, "one right after the other all around the tree."

Although we'd been warned not to expect many presents, we hung up our stockings anyway and hoped for the best. The best wasn't what we found in our stockings. It was the big surprise waiting for Mama. I saw it first.

The only day of the year that I was up before my parents was Christmas morning. I had been awake off and on all night wondering if Santa Claus would leave another delicious orange, and as soon as I dared, I went to see. I was able to sneak down from the barn loft, where I slept, without waking either Ed or George. The house was still dark, so I carefully lifted the glass chimney and lit the kerosene lamp.

I must have gasped when I saw the shine of wood and the dark designs of curved metal. Or maybe it was the light that woke Mama up. Anyway, before I knew it, she ran into the room. Then she saw it, too—the sewing machine.

"Oh!" she cried. "Oh!" She reached out and traced her finger around the wheel, and tears welled up in her eyes. "Oh!" she whispered, and pulled up a chair and sat down. She placed her feet on the treadle and tipped it slowly back and forth. The wheel turned; the needle went up and down. It was just like Grandma Cookson's sewing machine back in Utah.

Papa appeared in the doorway grinning like Alice in Wonderland's Cheshire cat.

"Oh, Albert!" Mama cried, and ran to hug him.

By then everyone in the house was awake, and soon Ed and George came in from the barn.

"I can't believe it!" Mama said, and looked with love at Papa. "But, Albert, we can't afford to . . ."

"Can't afford not to," Papa told her, "with a family that's growing like ours."

"But where? How?"

"One fireplace chimney," Papa explained, "over at Howes'."

So that's what Papa had been doing at the neighbors' while my brothers and I were working on Ed's chores.

"When?" Mama asked.

"When you weren't lookin'," Papa told her, and gave her a Christmas kiss.

We all dumped out the stockings we'd hung up the night before. In each were three pieces of candy twisted like a ribbon, a few nuts, a shiny nickel, and yes, another of those wonderful oranges. I wished, again, that I could have my own orange tree.

Caroline opened her present from me: the flour sack pillowcase I had embroidered with blue ribbons and pink bleeding hearts. Frank gave Ed some used horseshoes he'd painted white, and Ed gave Frank the post he was going to put in the ground to throw them over. Caroline and George had made a striped beanbag for Howard and a flowered one for Irene. Howard gave me a cardboard bookmark he'd decorated with pictures he'd cut out of the Sears Roebuck catalog. Irene's present for George was another beanbag—plain red on one side and blue on the other.

Papa took us outside to see what he'd done with the two long square posts he'd sunk solidly in the ground just far enough apart for him to reach between. Across the top another board had been nailed, and hanging from it was a rope with a wooden seat across the bottom. A swing! Even without money, we had lots of new things to play with.

During the holidays I made a Christmas quilt block with Mama's sewing machine on it and began the third reader. Then, quite by accident, I discovered how to do the handwriting exercises with my whole arm.

One evening when I was helping Mama with the dishes, I picked up a platter to dry and realized that I was making exactly the same round-and-round movements that we were supposed to practice for penmanship. And I was doing it with my arm! I pretended that I was holding a pen and whirled the dish towel around and around on one plate after the other—first to the left and then to the right. Then I wiped the flat cookie pans up and down at just the right slant for the push-pulls. I was anxious to try them with a pencil and paper as soon as the dishes were done.

It worked! My figures were not perfect, but they were much better than I'd ever done before. I just might learn to write neatly enough to satisfy fussy Mr. Stern! I couldn't wait to show Cora Beth.

I went over to her house first thing the next morning and she had something to show me, too. She'd been making doll clothes! We spent a good part of the vacation playing house and practicing penmanship together.

"Your handwriting looks much better," she said. "What are you doing differently?"

I told her about how I'd learned to use my whole arm.

We never visited each other on Sundays, however, because the Tracys belonged to the Baptist church and we attended the Church of Jesus Christ of Latter-day Saints that met in Clovis. Papa and the boys always hurried to finish the morning chores so we'd have plenty of time to ride the ten miles for morning Sunday School. After that, we'd go to the Lenstroms' for dinner, then return to the church for the afternoon meeting. We'd known the Lenstroms for as long as I could remember. Jenny and Sarah were the same ages as Caroline and I, and we became especially close when we traveled in the same wagon train from Utah. We enjoyed visiting with them every Sunday. They lived too far away to attend our school and had spent Thanksgiving with another family.

Both Christmas and New Year's Day were on Mondays that year. When we returned to school on Tuesday, I thought we'd come to the end of the holiday season. But before the week was out, there was news of another event to celebrate in New Mexico.

6

Forty-Seven-Star Flag

On Monday, January 6, 1912, New Mexico officially become the forty-seventh state. President William Howard Taft signed the proclamation at exactly 1:35 P.M. at the White House. The message was sent by telegraph.

To tell the truth, I'd forgotten that New Mexico wasn't a state yet. But Papa hadn't.

"It's about time," he said. "The New Mexican people have been trying for sixty years to convince the national government to grant them statehood. Fifty bills have been presented to Congress about it. Finally they approved one."

Miss Foster was excited about the news, too. "Next Fourth of July," she told us, "our star will be added to the United States flag. That will make forty-seven stars to go with the thirteen stripes." She assigned us to figure out a pattern for arranging forty-seven stars.

It was a challenge. Forty-seven was an uneven number that couldn't be divided by any other. What kind of design would be best? Circles? Squares? Staggered lines?

"You'd better make a plan for forty-eight stars, too," Miss Foster suggested. "Arizona should become a state pretty soon."

Forty-eight was easy. The same as my quilt pattern. Six rows one way and eight the other. I thought that maybe my next quilt block would be a flag with the same number of stars as my quilt had squares—or else one with forty-seven. It wasn't either, though. It was another square about another narrow escape.

One afternoon Miss Foster asked how many of us were born in New Mexico. Only three people raised their hands.

"That means that all the rest of you must have come from somewhere else," the teacher said. We nodded our heads. "Now that you live here, you should find out about your new state. For a while all of our lessons will have something to do with New Mexico. Then you'll pair off to do appropriate reports for extra credit. Think about what your project might be as we study the history."

She flipped through the big maps hanging on the

stand until she found the ones of North America and the United States. They were right next to each other, so she could flip quickly between them to locate any of the places she talked about. She wrote "SPELLING LIST (New Mexico)" on the board.

"Knowing how to spell these words," she said, "will give you extra points when I make up the report cards."

I needed all the extra credit I could get. I wrote "SPELLING LIST (New Mexico)" on my paper. The first unfamiliar word was *Pueblo*. That was the name of the Indians who were the original people to make their homes in our state. With a small *p*, it was also the name of their houses.

"They lived peacefully in villages," Miss Foster said, "grew crops, made pottery, and wove baskets. Sometimes they traveled all the way to Mexico along the oldest road ever made in our state. It is called the Turquoise Trail because the Indians took their sky-blue stones to trade for brightly colored parrot feathers found in Mexico and beautiful abalone shells from the Pacific Ocean."

Miss Foster's pointer followed the route across the map. Remembering our long trip from Utah, I wondered how many months it had taken the Pueblo Indians to travel so many miles. They didn't have covered wagons then, or even horses, Miss Foster told us. They walked all the way.

I made a note of "Turquoise Trail."

"They needed the feathers and shells," she said, "to make costumes for their religious ceremonies." She held up some pictures of people dressed in strange costumes, with horrible masks on their heads.

Frank looked back and smiled at Ed, two rows behind him, then faced forward and, for a change, paid close attention to what the teacher was saying.

Neither one of my brothers was as excited about learning new things as I was. Usually they fidgeted nervously in their seats during class discussion. But that day they listened.

"The Pueblos were guided by supernatural beings called 'kachinas,'" Miss Foster continued.

"Every year," she said, "the best dancers dressed up in beautiful costumes and wore elaborate masks to perform sacred ceremonies to please the kachinas. The clothes were always trimmed with feathers and sometimes with snakeskins or coyote and fox tails. The sacred kachina masks were made of deerskin, buffalo hide, or cowhide. Some, as you can see, had monstrous beaks, big horns, rolling eyes, huge eagle feather crowns, or buffalo, horse, or deer heads."

When Miss Foster showed another picture, Frank looked at Ed again and the boys nodded and grinned at each other. I knew they were in cahoots about something.

"Dancers were accompanied by drums, turtle shell rattles, and a chanting chorus that made gestures of falling rain," Miss Foster said, showing us what she meant. "Let's all stand up and try that," she suggested, looking from one of my restless brothers to the other.

While our fingers trickled down from above our heads, pretending to be rain, Miss Foster said, "The Indians always prayed for rain to make their crops grow."

So does Papa, I thought. *Maybe all farmers do.*

Miss Foster signaled us to be seated.

Frank got busy copying one of the masks, and even Ed started jotting something down.

"Kachina dolls," Miss Foster went on, "were also made to represent the gods. They were carved by men from cottonwood roots and used as children's toys or altar ornaments."

The boys had evidently heard all they wanted to when the teacher began talking about dolls. I could tell by the way he wiggled in his seat that Frank was itching to get out of the classroom.

Ed was squirming, too. "Sit still!" I hissed.

As soon as class was dismissed, both boys shot out of the door as if they'd been fired from a cannon. They hurried home so fast, I couldn't catch up. I was sure they meant to make themselves some of those ugly kachina masks.

I was right about that. I heard them whispering in

the barn while I was studying up in the hayloft.

"Did you get the wire?" Ed asked.

"Yup," Frank answered. "And some string. How about feathers?"

"Plenty. In the gunnysack."

"Could we use that old hog skull that Mama cooked the meat off of to make headcheese?"

"Maybe," Ed said. "But it's kinda small. What we really need is a shaggly, scraggly buffalo head."

"Yeah," Frank agreed, "but I don't know where we'd get one, do you?"

"Nope." Ed shook his head.

"Maybe we'll have to make one," Frank said.

I peeked over the edge of the hayloft. Frank was bending some wire.

"Come to think of it," Ed began, "I saw an old cowhide and some steer horns when I was over at Willie Pearce's."

"What color cow?"

"Black."

"That'd be okay. We could wire the horns on."

"Yeah."

"Think they'd let us have 'em?"

"Sure. They threw 'em away."

"We can ask."

"Yeah, they'll probably be glad to have 'em hauled off."

"Let's go."

The two boys rode the horse over to the Pearces' and on the way they must have collected everything else they needed. After their morning chores were done on Saturday, they worked almost all the rest of the day out behind the henhouse.

When I took the younger boys to see what they were doing, Ed sent us away.

"Don't come any closer," he warned as we approached. Then, his voice as sweet as sugar, he cooed, "We're making you a surprise."

"Yeah," Frank agreed, "don't spoil it."

Howard and George ran back to the house, but I hesitated just around the corner of the chicken coop and overheard Ed remark, "They'll have a *big* surprise, all right."

"I'll say." Frank snickered. "We'll scare the living daylights out of them."

Those boys thought it would be funny to frighten their little brothers with their hideous masks! I thought it was mean.

Late in the afternoon, Mama sent me out to gather the eggs. I could hear Ed and Frank talking. They must have finished making the masks.

"Okay," I heard Frank say through the henhouse wall, "put it on me."

"It's heavy." Ed groaned.

"That's all right," Frank told him. "I have a strong neck."

Then I heard a thud and a muffled voice saying, "It's too tight. I can't breathe! Take it off."

"Calm down," Ed said.

"Hurry," Frank coaxed frantically.

"Calm down," Ed insisted firmly. "It's stuck."

I didn't wait to hear any more. Remembering the time we nearly killed Ed on the hog hoist, I ran to the field screaming for Papa. Everyone else heard, too, I guess, because by the time we came racing back they were all out behind the henhouse with Ed and Frank.

"Hurry, Albert," Mama begged. "Do something. Frank's smothering in there."

"Then we'll just have to give him a little air," Papa said calmly, and pulled out his pocket knife.

"Don't move, Frank," he said in a voice loud enough to be heard through the thick, mangy mask. "I'm cutting an airhole."

Slowly, carefully, Papa nibbled at the hairy hide with his knife until he made a slit. We could hear our brother sucking the air in muffled gasps. He wasn't dead yet.

Gradually, Papa exposed Frank's frightened face, reassuring him over and over that everything was going to be all right. "Now to get this smelly thing off," Papa said, trying to lift it up.

"Stop!" Frank screamed. "You're ripping my ear off."

Sure enough, a wire was caught below his ear and was slicing into his skin. It took a long time for Papa to cut and clip and pull the mask apart enough to get it away from Frank's head. By then both boys had had enough of kachina masks. Ed wouldn't even put his on.

"What on earth were you boys doing?" Papa wanted to know.

"Schoolwork," Ed said.

"What kind of schoolwork is this?" Papa asked, shaking his head.

"Our extra-credit project about New Mexico history," Frank said. He gave a good explanation of kachinas.

"It sounds like you really learned that lesson," Papa said, "in more ways than one."

Later, at supper, Howard asked, "Where's our surprise, Ed?"

"Not finished yet," Ed told him, and I knew he was trying to figure out a different kind of surprise than the one he'd originally had in mind.

George and Howard kept bothering the older boys about the surprise. Ed finally had to bribe Caroline to make some oatmeal cookies for them.

"I'll make faces on them with raisins," Ed volunteered.

Caroline didn't mind. She loved to cook. She didn't like to sew or work in the yard, but she was always happy in the kitchen. She even liked to do housework. And read. Whenever she finished cleaning, she buried her nose in a book until it was time to help with the next meal.

I think Miss Foster would have been pleased that the boys made the masks, because she thought the best way to learn about things was to try them out. I told Ed he should take his to school for extra credit.

"Pooh," he said. "Who needs extra credit?"

"You do," I said.

"Who cares?" he growled. "School's nothing but a pain in the neck!"

"Yeah," Frank said, rubbing a tender spot. "*My* neck."

School wasn't a pain for me. I loved it. Even if the boys wouldn't take their masks to show the teacher, I told Miss Foster what they did.

"That's very ingenious," Miss Foster said. "Maybe those boys will soak up some information about our state after all."

Mama was sewing up a storm with her new machine. We had received a big box full of outgrown clothes from Aunt Zoe, back in Utah. Mama turned them into dresses for me, Caroline, and Irene, and made shirts for the boys and a new coat for Howard. We each had something new to wear to church. Mama taught me to use the machine to make doll clothes with the scraps.

The quilt blocks were all done by hand. I made one with a picture of Frank wearing his mask. I found a small piece of hairy cowhide to stitch on for the head, but it was too stiff to sew through. I had to settle for a brown scrap of fuzzy wool left over from Howard's coat.

7

My Favorite Time of Day

I loved learning about New Mexico. Miss Foster spent mornings working with each grade separately on reading, writing, and arithmetic or listening to fourth grade poetry recitations. But in the afternoon, the whole room studied together about our new state. To make sure we understood how the ancient Indians did things, Miss Foster taught us how to do what they did. We were allowed to choose partners, so Cora Beth and I worked as a team.

It was my favorite time of day. When all the classes joined in on the same project, I didn't feel so far behind everyone my own age. I loved making things, and even more, I enjoyed being with my friend. We really did feel like sisters. Every day, catching up to my grade became more important to me. When I did,

Cora Beth and I could study the same lessons all the time.

One day Miss Foster showed us how to melt dried adobe bricks into soft clay by adding just the right amount of water. Each of us kneaded a lumpy mass like bread dough until it was smooth and silky. We used the clay to make models of the terraced houses where Pueblo Indians lived. The flat dwellings, stacked one on top of the other, had no doors or windows where enemies could enter. The only openings were holes in the tops for smoke from their fires to escape. The Indians entered and left their homes through the same holes.

When we finished the pueblos, we used the leftover clay to make pottery bowls, cups, and cooking pots the way the Indians did long ago. We rolled pieces of clay into ropes, coiled them on top of each other to make the right shapes, then smoothed the cords together with wet fingers.

When we were done, Cora Beth flattened a scrap of the soft clay and cut out a small heart. With her pencil she marked an *X* with a circle around it. I knew that meant a kiss and a hug. On the other side she wrote "I LOVE YOU." Then she handed the heart to me. "For good luck," she whispered.

I made one for her, too. With my baby finger, I pressed a forget-me-not on top by making one dent for the center and five around it for the petals. I inscribed "FORGET-ME-NOT" on the back. "To remember me by," I told her.

"Let's make a hole in each one to put a ribbon through," Cora Beth suggested. "Then we can hang our hearts around our necks if we want to."

Several days later, after our projects had dried, Miss Foster asked us, "What would happen, now, if you put water in your cups and bowls?"

"They would melt," I blurted out.

"You are quite right," Miss Foster said. "After their pots dried, the Indians had to cook them for a long time in their fires. That hardened them permanently so they wouldn't turn back into clay when they got wet."

"We need to cook our hearts so they'll last forever," I whispered to Cora Beth.

"Good idea," she agreed. "We wouldn't want our luck to run out in the first rainstorm."

When Papa was burning some bear grass he'd cleared from a new field, I asked if we could bake our hearts.

"Sure," he said. "Put them in a pie tin so they won't get lost in the ashes, and I'll see that they get fired."

The cooking darkened the clay but it made our charms waterproof. We kept them in our desks so we could trade them back and forth for good luck whenever we faced a particular challenge.

After we made the cooking pots, we studied about fierce, wandering Apaches, who lived in wikiups. They could roll them up to take with them when they moved.

Cora Beth and I made buckskin clothes for our dolls with some tan scraps we found in the ragbag. We trimmed them, Apache style, with some of the tiny beads I'd brought in a slim bottle when we moved from Utah. Next we made cradle boards so we could carry our "papooses" on our backs. We used them for our extra-credit projects.

We learned about the peaceful Navajos, who built hogans shaped like beehives. They settled down in one place and raised corn and sheep.

"Navajos made rugs, didn't they?" I asked Miss Foster.

"Indeed they did, Dora. They wove them from wool. How did you know that?"

"I heard Papa say so when we met some on the way to New Mexico."

In our after-school session that day, Miss Foster said, "You have a remarkable memory, Dora. You're always coming up with something that surprises me. How do you do it?"

"Easy," I told her. "I just don't forget."

She chuckled. "So I've noticed."

"I *had* to keep things straight in my head before I learned to talk. I guess I can still do it," I told her.

"Have you ever done any memorizing?" Miss Foster asked.

"All the nursery rhymes," I said. "And church songs."

"How about reciting?"

"Oh, no, I'd be too scared to do that."

"It's not much different than spelling a word in front of the class," my teacher said.

"That's *awful*!" I told her.

"But you're getting much better at it," she assured me.

Miss Foster changed the subject to something else, but I knew what she had in mind. All fourth graders were required to learn and recite long poems by famous authors. She seemed to think I could do that. A little shiver climbed up my backbone. Was it fear? Or excitement? Some of both, I'm sure.

Before I started memorizing, though, Miss Foster decided it was time I quit using a pencil to practice penmanship.

"Your writing has improved so much since Christmas," she said, "I think you should try pen and ink."

"Only fourth graders do that," I said.

"That's true," she replied with a look that indicated I'd already skipped over grade three, "so you need to do it." It was a disaster.

The ink dripped onto the paper in huge, ugly blots. Only pages with no smears could be turned in, and each sheet had to be filled from top to bottom before I was allowed to have a clean one. Miss Foster showed me that each time the pen was dipped into the ink, the tip had to be wiped against the top of the inkwell to remove the extra liquid.

No matter how much I reminded myself, I forgot often enough that I dropped a blot at least once on every sheet of paper. Writing a perfect page seemed impossible. Then one Friday when I got home from school, I noticed Howard stringing painted spools on a long leather bootlace. "Red, blue, white," he sang, "red, blue, white," to remind him which color spool to put on next.

Soon I was singing with him. "Red, blue, white. Red, blue, white." If I just had a short refrain like that about wiping the pen point, I could sing it again and again every time I wrote.

"Red, blue, white," I sang. "Dip, wipe, write." That was the right idea to describe the action: *dip* the pen, *wipe* off the drip, begin to *write.* But the words tangled around my tongue when I said them fast. They got all mixed up with each other, as if I were stuttering. I didn't want to start that again.

I tried another combination: "Dip, drip, write." That was it! "Dip, drip, write." The words flowed easily no matter how many times I repeated them.

"Dip, drip, write," I sang. I picked up a pencil, dipped it into a tin cup full of water, wiped off the excess, and wrote my name on the table. I could practice without pen or ink. Maybe by the end of the year I'd have a perfect page of writing to show Mr. Stern.

In the meantime, I'd make good use of all those wasted sheets of paper by using the poems I needed to memorize for my penmanship practice. Writing them down would help me learn them. If the pages were nice enough, I could turn them in to the teacher.

Even if I could write with an ink pen, though, I'd never be able to make a map.

Miss Foster always encouraged us to use our imaginations, and that was something I was good at. But my inventiveness turned out to be a big problem when the teacher decided I needed to know something about geography. I hated the tedious business of trying to draw the maps she assigned me. So I used my imagination. I changed the shapes of rivers, lakes, and borders to suit my fancy. If a stream wound around to remind me of a face, I made it into a face. If a lake looked a little like a fat pig, I couldn't resist drawing ears and a curly tail. It was wonderful fun but hardly what Miss Foster had in mind.

No matter how many times she asked me to try again, I just could *not* copy a map—especially a coastline like Greece or Chile. It drove me crazy.

Neither could I figure out ups and downs on a flat map. Hills and valleys, mesas and mountains all looked the same. To me, north was up and south was down because that's the way those directions went when the maps hung from their stand in the classroom. Besides, people always talked about "up north" or "down south." It made sense to me because Utah, which was north of New Mexico, had lots of high mountains while south of there, our homestead land was flat as a pancake. For the same reason, it seemed to me that all rivers flowed south, too, because water would just naturally run downhill from the top of a map. When Miss Foster told me that the Nile River ran north, I couldn't believe it.

I remembered when we were moving to New Mexico and I followed the map with Papa. All the roads went up and down and wound around, but when he pointed to them on the map, they were just flat, not-very-wiggly lines. Just a short distance on a piece of paper stretched into a long day's travel. I wondered, even then, what a map really told about a place. Not much, it seemed to me. But being able to draw one could make the difference between skipping a grade or staying where I was. I needed to know how.

8

Seven Cities of Cíbola

I could hardly wait for the end of each school day, when our teacher told us real stories about New Mexico history. At the appointed time, we'd put our books and papers away and Miss Foster would begin in her most beguiling voice.

"Imagine that you are a young Spaniard living in the 1500s," she began. "Your countryman, Columbus, has discovered a new land—America! Cortés has conquered Mexico and sent back promising reports to Spain of priceless treasures and valuable property. Gold and precious stones are everywhere, so the rumor goes.

"Soon a tale is told of seven golden cities, the Cities of Cíbola, cities so rich that the streets are paved with gold. The natives, it is said, have so many diamonds and precious metals that they can hardly carry their ornaments with them. Their houses are studded with turquoise. Even the poorest people eat on plates of pure gold."

Plates of pure gold, I thought. I imagined opening our cupboard to see all that gold.

"In your mind the gold begins to glow," the teacher continued. "You think of the glory you could achieve by becoming rich, by converting the savages to Christianity. *Gold! Glory! And God!* You sail to America and, in February of 1540, with more than three hundred others, you join an expedition led by Coronado to find the fabulous cities.

"Your army consists of well-trained men carrying an assortment of weapons, even some cannons. Officers are dressed in gleaming armor, plumed hats, and brilliant red-and-yellow capes. They are mounted on horseback. A hundred Mexican Indians follow your army to carry supplies, tend the livestock, and do the work when camp is set up in the evenings. There are three women in the company. One of them is a nurse."

I imagined I was the nurse. Like Florence Nightingale, I would comfort and care for the soldiers no matter what happened to them.

"Your splendid army rides north through Mexico full of high hopes," Miss Foster continued, following the route on the map with her pointer.

"Traveling with such a large group is slow. You have to climb high mountains where pack animals slip and fall."

I would be there with iodine and bandages.

"You cross rivers with no bridges. People get sick, and two die from eating poisonous plants."

What could a nurse, even Florence Nightingale, do about poisonous plants?

"Horses go lame," the teacher continued. "Food is hard to find; the Indians you see are not friendly. The journey is harder than anyone thought. In April, you are part of a smaller band that is chosen to go ahead of the others to find the fabled golden cities.

"April passes, then May. Now you are in Arizona with its hot, dry deserts. Still your goal is somewhere ahead of you. How far? You do not know. June comes. The summer sizzles."

Miss Foster stopped her story for a moment. "Did any of you cross a desert when you moved to New Mexico?" she asked. Almost every hand went up.

"In the summer?" A few indicated they had.

"What was it like?"

"Hot!" Cora Beth said.

"Terrible," Toby added.

"I wondered if we'd ever get to the end," Gertie said.

"The Spanish explorers must have wondered the same thing," Miss Foster went on. "But finally, sometime in July, what do you think occurred?"

I could tell by the way she asked the question that Miss Foster wanted us to think about it for a while.

"Tonight," she continued, "use your imaginations to make up an ending to this story and then write it down. Tomorrow, we'll find out what really happened."

As I walked home, I remembered how we had left Utah with such high hopes for a place of our own in New Mexico. I was expecting to find a green Garden of Eden with trees and grass and flower beds like Grandpa Cookson's place in Holladay. I had looked forward to acres and acres of watermelon plants. Instead we found a weedy wilderness covered with cactus, and a run-down shack instead of a house.

Mama's rainbow gave us hope again. Papa fixed up the shack and added some rooms. We planted a garden and grew our first crop of broomcorn. We'd never heard of that kind of corn, but found out that the dried tassels were used to make brooms in the factory in Texico. We were still climbing uphill, but we were going to make it.

I could imagine how Coronado must have felt in the hot, dry July desert. His eyes must have been stiff with looking. His heart must have been tired of hoping. Maybe he was discouraged. Maybe he doubted if the stories he'd heard were true.

How should I write the end of the story? Did the

magnificent men in the Spanish expedition find so much treasure they couldn't carry it home? Or were they weary and ragged and dirty from months and months of tiresome traveling? Did they find the same thing in New Mexico that we did? Not very much?

I couldn't decide what to write. My heart hoped for a happy ending. My mind told me it was impossible.

In the end I tried to be funny:

Coronado found Cíbola
Sizzling in the sun;
Wanted water more than gold
Before the day was done.

Miss Foster didn't leave us wondering what really happened this time. She actually told us. But not until after she'd read our made-up endings to the story.

"Some of you," she said, "have vivid imaginations, some a true talent for telling a story, and one or two showed real insight. Listen to this." Then she read my poem!

"Instead of a city gleaming with golden streets, and wealthy people wearing jewels," Miss Foster told us, "Coronado's party found six dingy adobe houses and a few Zuni Indians with barely enough food to keep themselves alive. They surely didn't find what they were looking for, but they had found the place that eventually became New Mexico. In time, the Spanish conquered most of the Indians who lived here.

"Later, the Anglos, or other white races, came from the east and north. First it was the trappers looking for furs. Then traders bringing goods to sell. Cattle ranchers moved over from Texas and soon homesteaders were coming from everywhere. So you see why so many different kinds of people live here."

Miss Foster changed the second grade arithmetic problems so they added or subtracted squash, ears of corn, or tortillas. The third graders figured out how many Spanish gold pieces, silver bracelets, or beaver furs it took to buy guns or bullets or other goods brought by traders from the east.

Fourth graders figured out how far the merchants had to travel along the Santa Fe Trail. From Independence, Missouri, where the roadway started, to the end at Santa Fe was 780 miles. That wasn't as far as our family had traveled from Utah to Clovis.

We'd been studying about New Mexico ever since Christmas vacation. Already Valentine's Day had come and gone. That was baby Irene's first birthday, and the day Arizona became a state. Now there never would be a forty-seven-star flag. I was glad I hadn't made one on a quilt block.

March came in like a lamb, bringing weather warm enough for us girls to get out the jump rope and for the boys to fill their pockets with marbles. By now, Miss Foster had started in earnest to prepare us for the annual spelling bee, the one that decided who would represent our class in the county spell-down on March 30. While Ed and the boys tried to win the most marbles playing keeps, Cora Beth and I practiced spelling to the beat of our jumping. Lucy and Mary Jane joined us as well, now that the final competition was approaching.

Cora Beth and I said the letters out loud in the afternoons, too, sometimes walking home to her house, sometimes to mine. We knew the school list backwards and forwards and sideways so our parents hunted up unfamiliar words in newspapers, books, and even Cora Beth's dictionary, a gift from her grandma who lived in Georgia. Using the sounds of the letters and the rules we'd learned, we were supposed to be able to figure out how to spell almost any word.

When the big day finally came, we felt like we were prepared for anything. But, for me, the whole thing turned out to be an enormous disaster—D-I-S-A-S-T-E-R.

Actually, *losing* the spelling bee wasn't the problem. Everyone knew that Cora Beth Tracy was the best speller in the room and that she deserved to win. It was the way I lost that was so humiliating.

For just a second, when there were only two of us left

standing in front of the class, with Cora Beth spelling one word and me the next, I had the idea that I might beat her—that a second grader might possibly win over a fourth grader. Quicker than a wink, I had the thought that, if I did, it would prove to everyone that I was smart enough to skip two more grades.

In that moment, I must have lost my concentration. We'd sailed through all the New Mexico words without a miss, and the others were getting more difficult. When my turn came and I heard the word I was to spell, all I could think was, *Easy, easy, easy. That word is so easy.*

"Embarrassing," I repeated, and said the letters I was so sure of even faster than usual. "E-M-B-A-R-R-A-S-I-N-G. Embarrass . . ."

I felt my face blaze fiery red. No one needed to tell me that I'd left out the second *s*. All I'd proved was that I was stupid. Very stupid.

I sat down at my desk and ducked my head, wishing an instant hole would open up for me to drop through. What a word to miss on! *Embarrassing*. Yes, it was. And would be forever. Very embarrassing.

"Embarrassing," I heard Cora Beth repeat, and the word burned like a branding iron in my ears. "E-M-B-A-R-R-A-S-*S*-I-N-G," she spelled slowly, deliberately, emphasizing the second *s*. "Embarrassing." The same word that was my disgrace was her glory.

Cora Beth was my best friend. I couldn't be sorry she won the spelling bee. But that didn't keep me from being embarrassed.

Miss Foster congratulated her and gave her the blue ribbon. She praised me for making so much progress in less than a year, and gave me the red. But that didn't keep me from being embarrassed, either. My face was the same color as my ribbon.

"It's okay," Ed encouraged me on the way home. "You can win next year when Cora Beth is in Mr. Stern's room."

Ed didn't know yet that I intended to be in Mr. Stern's room, too, by next year.

After that, Cora Beth kept right on practicing for the big Roosevelt County competition she would participate in at Portales on March 30.

Before the spell-down, however, something happened that changed everything.

9

The White Satin Bed

As soon as Cora Beth got to school on Wednesday, I could tell that she wasn't feeling very well because she sat down on the steps, hugging her stomach, instead of running in the back door of the jump rope without even stopping to see how fast we were turning it. No matter how hard I practiced, I couldn't do that without counting out the beat of the rope several times first. But Cora Beth always did. Except this day she didn't. She sat on the step.

I asked Gertie to take my end of the rope and went over to Cora Beth.

"What's the matter?" I asked.

"Nothing much," she said, "just a stomachache. I'll feel better by recess."

She acted the same as usual during class. Either she

felt better or else she was trying not to let anyone know that she was ill. I decided that her pain must be gone.

But at recess she was sitting on the step again. She alternately held her breath and took short gasps as if it didn't hurt so much when she breathed that way.

"You should tell the teacher," I told her. "Maybe she'll let you go home."

"No!" she insisted. "I've never missed a day of school in my life because I was sick, and I'm not going to start now."

That's when I got the feeling that *I* ought to tell Miss Foster, but when I told Cora Beth, she said, "Don't you dare! I'll be all right." So I didn't.

Mama says I should pay attention to ideas like that. "There's always a reason you have those feelings," she says. "You don't always find out what it is if you obey them, but if you *don't* you're sure to see why you should have. By then it's too late."

Cora Beth agreed that I could tell the teacher if she felt any worse by noon. She did, and I told Miss Foster. The teacher put her hand against Cora Beth's forehead to see if it was hot and asked her if she wanted to go home. Cora Beth shook her head.

"Not yet," she said weakly. I couldn't believe she said that.

"Maybe you'll feel better if you lie down for a while," Miss Foster suggested.

Cora Beth nodded and curled up on the recitation bench in the front of the classroom. Miss Foster tucked a rolled-up sweater under her head for a pillow and covered her with a coat. "When I have a pain," she said, "I always want a hot water bottle on it."

She looked around the room as if she'd find something to use. She did. It was the lid off the potbellied stove where the early-morning fire had died down. She scraped the thick black soot off the bottom, wrapped the heavy circle in a clean rag, and placed the warm package next to Cora Beth's stomach.

"There," she said, "doesn't that feel better?"

"I guess so," Cora Beth said.

"We'll leave you alone while we go outside for lunch, and we'll lock the door so no one will disturb you," the teacher said. "Try to take a little nap."

When Miss Foster unlocked the door an hour later, Cora Beth was waiting inside doubled over in pain.

"I think I'm gonna die." She groaned. "Please, can I go home?"

"Maybe you'd better," Miss Foster said. "You look awful."

I offered to go with her, but my friend insisted she'd be all right.

When Cora Beth started off across the school lot, I waved good-bye. She lifted a weak arm, turned her fingers down a little, and said, "I hope I see you again."

I thought she really must feel terrible, to say a thing like that.

When I got home I told Mama I hoped Cora Beth would be better in time for the spelling bee.

"Is she sick?" she asked.

"She had a bad stomachache and had to go home," I said.

"Probably something she ate. She'll be back in the morning," Mama assured me.

But she wasn't back in the morning, and the teacher didn't look very well herself. I thought Cora Beth must have something catching.

Miss Foster pulled her hanky out of the top drawer, held it to her nose, and cleared her throat two or three times. She could hardly talk. She struggled to control her voice, but it cracked anyway.

Cora Beth Tracy was dead.

Dead. I couldn't believe it. My heart felt as if it had stopped, and the blood drained down into my feet. My brain went numb from the shock. *Dead.* I heard the word, but it seemed faint and far away. Flat and final. Heavy and hard. And cold.

I don't know what happened next. I was too dazed to notice. But after a while, Miss Foster straightened her shoulders, took a deep breath, and attempted to get on with school as usual. She tried hard, but she couldn't concentrate, and neither could the rest of us. Just before morning recess, when she started to write the new spelling words on the board, her hand trembled so much she could hardly hold the chalk. She stopped in the middle of a word and turned to face us. Tears were streaming down her cheeks.

"It's no use!" She choked. "I can't do it. You might as well go home." She put her head down on her desk and sobbed as if her heart would break. Without a word, we put our books away and filed from the room.

I walked home in a fog of disbelief. When I got there, Mama was already working on the burial dress. I recognized the white material.

"That was supposed to be Cora Beth's Easter dress!" I choked.

"Yes," Mama agreed. "Mrs. Tracy had it all cut out. It's going to be beautiful with rows of tucks and lace down the front and pink flowers embroidered in the middle." She'd already stitched the tucks with her machine.

"How come *you're* making it?" I asked.

"I offered to," she said.

"You went over there?" I asked, wondering what you'd to say to somebody whose little girl had just died.

"Of course," she said. "As soon as I heard."

"Weren't you scared?"

"Scared of what?"

"Scared of going," I said, not sure what I meant.

"Of course not," she said. "As many times as you've been over there, would you be scared?"

"Probably," I admitted. "I wouldn't know what to say."

"What you say isn't as important as being there," she told me. "What matters is showing that you care."

I picked up another piece of white material from the table. It was cut the same shape as Cora Beth's dress but much smaller. It had tucks stitched, too.

"What's this?" I asked.

"That's for Cora Beth's doll," Mama said.

"Why?" I choked. "She can't play with it anymore."

"Rose Marie's going to be buried with her," Mama told me, "in a matching dress."

The last time Cora Beth and I played with our dolls, they were dressed in matching dresses—beaded buckskin clothes like the Apaches wore. They were tied in their cradle boards strapped to our backs.

"Can I make the doll dress?" I asked.

"I think your friend would like that," she said.

While Mama and I sat side by side hand-sewing the lace to the edges of the tucks, I talked to her about what had happened the day before.

"It made me feel funny," I told her, "the way Cora Beth said, 'I *hope* I see you again.' Do you think she knew she was going to die?"

"She probably felt like she might," Mama said.

"I've felt that way once or twice."

"You have? When?"

"When I had a terrible pain that wouldn't go away."

I stopped sewing because my eyes were too full of tears to see. "I'm glad *you* didn't die," I whispered.

"Me too," she agreed.

We talked some more about dying, and Mama told me about how nice it was up in heaven and that we'd all see Cora Beth again someday. I felt a little better when I went outside to talk to Papa.

I told him the same thing I'd told Mama, and when I got to the part about the warm stove lid, he exploded.

"Warm?" he cried. "Doesn't Miss Foster know that you never put heat on a stomachache?"

"Why not?" I asked him.

"Because it might be appendicitis," Papa said. "And it was. And it killed her."

"Did the stove lid make it worse?" I wanted to know.

"Yes," Papa said, "and so did the long walk home from school. But mostly it was not getting to the doctor soon enough. He didn't operate in time."

"But Miss Foster didn't know." I defended my teacher. "It wasn't her fault."

"No," Papa agreed.

"And Cora Beth didn't know. It wasn't her fault."

"No," Papa said in a tired voice. "It wasn't anyone's

fault. No one knew how serious it was until it was too late."

I knew whose fault it was. Mine. I hadn't paid any attention to the feeling that I should tell the teacher earlier. If I had, Cora Beth might still be alive.

On Friday everyone in our class was making crepe-paper flowers to take to the funeral. Blue flowers. Roses. Blue roses.

No matter how carefully I rolled the edges around a knitting needle or stretched the centers of the petals to make them cup a little, no matter how nicely I curled them around each other, they didn't look like roses. The color was all wrong. Roses are orange and red and yellow. They are pink and white. But not blue. Never blue. Roses are happy colors. Not sad, like blue. Forget-me-nots are blue.

School was dismissed early so the whole class could attend the services. I didn't want to go, but I did anyway. Mama said it was important to be there. At the last moment, I took the forget-me-not heart from Cora Beth's desk and slipped it into my pocket.

Our class walked in a solemn line all the way from school to the Tracys' house carrying the dreary blue roses. Even the sky was sad. Gloomy gray clouds stretched across the sun, cutting out the light. I had a stitch in my side long before we got there, and I thought about Cora Beth walking so far with the terrible pain in her stomach the day she died.

We climbed up the front steps and filed into the parlor where my adopted sister was lying in her coffin. We were supposed to walk by, single file, to see her for the last time.

I had never seen anyone who was dead before and especially didn't want to look at Cora Beth that way. But I did want to see if Rose Marie was there wearing the dress I'd made, so I planned to take a quick peek and hurry by when my turn came.

I hesitated a moment and took a deep breath before I moved ahead toward the casket. Just then the tender touch of a hand on my shoulder told me that Miss Foster was going to walk with me.

She squeezed gently to give me courage, and we proceeded together to the coffin.

Cora Beth was beautiful. Her dark hair was curled in perfect ringlets and tied with a new pink ribbon to match the flowers on her dress. She looked as if she was all ready to go to church and just fell asleep while she was waiting to be picked up. No wonder she dozed off, lying in that elegant bed of sleek and shiny satin. The quilted lining of the coffin cuddled around Cora Beth like a soft white cloud. It must feel like heaven itself, I decided, to sleep in a bed that soft. Except that someone who was dead couldn't tell how nice it felt, could she?

Cora Beth's doll was tucked in the corner of one arm, and I was glad Rose Marie was a shut-eye doll, because she was asleep, too. The dresses looked perfect and all my embroidery stitches were small and even. In Cora Beth's other hand was the blue ribbon she won at the spelling bee. She was so proud of that ribbon.

Miss Foster kept squeezing my shoulder, and I felt her tears dripping like rain on the top of my head. When I looked up at her face, it showed how much she was hurting. Maybe feelings of guilt were tying a hard knot in her stomach—a knot about the size of a warm stove lid wrapped in a piece of clean cloth. I wondered how many people had already told her that she should never put heat on a stomachache. I grabbed Miss Foster in a hug around her waist to let her know that I knew it wasn't her fault. She hugged back as if it wasn't mine, either.

Miss Foster's tears falling on my head reminded me that I hadn't been able to shed any tears yet. They had welled up in my eyes a few times, but none had fallen. I couldn't figure out why.

I reached in my pocket for the clay heart and rubbed it between my fingers to feel the indentions that made the forget-me-not. I tucked it carefully under the blue ribbon in Cora Beth's cold, stiff hand. "I'll never forget you," I whispered.

Finally, Miss Foster led me away so the long line of people waiting behind us could move ahead.

The schoolchildren followed the teacher from the Tracy home to the church down the street. We sat and listened to the sad organ music until it was time for the funeral to begin. My sweaty hands were green from the paper wrapped around the stems of my blue roses. We had been instructed to hold them until it was time to place them on the grave at the cemetery.

I thought about what Mama had said about listening to feelings. *If* I had told the teacher sooner and *if* Miss Foster had let Cora Beth go home and *if* the doctor had operated in time, I never would have known that I had saved her life. But because I didn't, Miss Foster didn't and the doctor didn't. I certainly knew why I should have obeyed that whispering in my mind.

Finally the pallbearers walked in carrying the small casket with a blanket of pink store-bought carnations on top. Everyone stood up until the family sat down in the front rows that had been saved for them, and the service began.

10

Trying to Get My Attention

I didn't hear what anyone said at the funeral. I thought a lot about the puffy satin lining of the coffin. I decided it was a nice thing to do for a person who had gone to sleep forever—to bury her in a nice soft bed. Even though she couldn't enjoy it, it made the rest of us feel better than if her beautiful body had been put into a bare box. I wondered if my sister would have a cozy, cuddly bed in heaven, maybe one made of clouds. I hoped so.

Before long, the talking stopped and the music started again. The pallbearers carried the coffin to the graveyard behind the church. I gave my horrid blue roses to Ed and headed for home. I didn't want to see dirt falling on the pretty pink coffin with my friend inside. The thought of leaving Cora Beth in a smothery grave was more than I could stand. I had to get away from there before that happened.

Suddenly, as I ran away from the cemetery, the tears I had been unable to shed began pouring out. Once I started to cry, I couldn't stop. After a long time, some of the sorrow seemed to wash away and I became angry instead.

"Why," I screamed up at the darkening sky, "did Cora Beth have to die? She was so pretty and smart and good. She was the Tracys' only girl in a family with all those boys. She always did what she was supposed to do and never caused anyone any trouble. Why should *she* die? Why not some no-account mean bully boy? Why not Toby Tully? No one would miss him."

I was mad at God for letting Cora Beth die. Although I was used to talking to him about almost everything, I'd never been upset with him before. I scolded for a long time like a boiling teakettle shooting out steam. Finally I had said all I wanted to say several times over. After a while, just like a fire dies down under a teakettle and the steam stops, my anger subsided.

A jagged bolt of lightning shot through the clouds. Thunder rumbled and the sky began to cry. The storm moved closer and closer until the crackles and the crashes came together like a big box of dynamite going off one stick at a time. A wild wind came up and whipped the rain in angry streaks. It seemed like God was trying to get my attention to explain his side of things.

The rain poured in torrents, soaking me to the skin, plastering my hair flat against my head and washing the green stain from my hands. It felt good. Like I was being lashed with a whip for not obeying my feelings to tell the teacher about Cora Beth's stomachache. Maybe, if I was punished enough, my mistake would be paid for and I could forget about it. I hoped Miss Foster could forget hers, too.

I walked home the long way, trying to sort out my thoughts. By the time I got there the storm was over; the sun was shining and I felt better.

Then I noticed a little miracle by the back step. The forget-me-nots were blooming! Mama had planted the stickery seeds the first year we were in New Mexico. "To remind me of home," she had said.

Though the plants had sprouted and the leaves grew thick and green, no blossoms came.

"Why not?" I asked her.

"They are biennials," she had said, "and won't bloom until the second year."

Now the plants were covered with dainty blue flowers. Forget-me-nots. Just the right thing to leave on Cora Beth's grave. They were beautiful with the lavender pansies blooming next to them. I picked a handful of both and walked back to the cemetery.

The soggy paper roses with blue and green dye leaking out on the muddy mound looked so awful that I picked them all up and threw them on the trash heap. I wrote Cora Beth's initials next to mine in the wet dirt and drew a heart around them. I decided to fix the flowers in the same shape on top.

I gathered enough green leaves to cover the spot and found three pink carnations that had dropped from the coffin bouquet. I put them in a triangle in the middle of the heart with the pansies tucked in between. I made a blue border all around the edge with the forget-me-nots. A white bow would have looked nice, but I didn't have a ribbon.

It seemed like my friend might be watching me and smiling because I fixed the flowers that way. Mama said her spirit would stay close until after she was buried. I hoped it was still around. Just in case, I decided to talk to her for a while.

"I'm glad you won the spelling bee," I told her. "I'll get another chance to do it. But"—my voice caught on a sob—"you never will."

I said thanks for being my friend and my sister, for teaching me all the fourth grade spelling words, and for showing me how to run in the back door of the jump rope. I talked about our pretend papooses with the Apache clothes and cradle boards. I promised to keep the heart-shaped good-luck piece she gave me. "I love you," I said, choking on the same words she'd written on the back.

I said I was sorry that I didn't tell the teacher to let her go home sooner the day she was so sick. I told her that I thought maybe God needed her up in heaven to be kind to someone who was lonesome, just like she had been so nice to me when I was new at school. That's probably the reason she died, I said, because God needed her.

After I finished talking to my friend, I started home. I kept thinking about everything that had happened. And about the white satin lining in the coffin that was such a waste because no one got to enjoy it while they were still alive.

Everyone else in my family was home from the meal that was served at the church after the funeral, but I wasn't ready to talk to them yet. I went into the barn through the back door and climbed up to the loft to change my wet clothes. I wanted to be alone for a while.

Henrietta smiled at me from the cradle board where she was hanging on the wall by my bed. I wondered what Mrs. Tracy had done with the buckskin dress and cradle board when she took them off to put the white burial dress on Cora Beth's doll. Did she throw them away because she couldn't stand to look at them? Or did she keep them?

I unwound the straps that held my doll and changed the beaded dress for a flannel nightgown. It made me sad to look at the Apache things, but I couldn't get rid of them. I put them in the treasure box where I kept my precious things.

I tucked Henrietta under the quilt with her head on my pillow so she'd be there to hug when I went to bed. I thought about the beautiful silky white bed where Cora Beth would sleep forever.

After a while, I climbed slowly down the ladder to go into the house and face the family.

Irene grabbed my legs and reached to be picked up. Caroline smiled a sad smile. Mama hugged me around the shoulders.

"You've been crying," she whispered, and I nodded. "That's good," she said.

The boys looked up from their game on the floor.

"Wanna play Old Maid?" Ed asked.

"Not yet," I told him.

"Then come outside with me," Papa said, "to see if the rain did any damage."

So I did. I carried my baby sister cuddled in my arms. Sweet little Irene was more precious than ever now that Cora Beth was gone.

When school started again the Monday after the funeral, it was clear that Miss Foster was still not feeling like her usual happy self. It was a difficult day for all of us. Finally our classes were over and the others had gone home.

"You and I need to work on these," Miss Foster said quietly, pulling the long list of spelling words out of her desk drawer. Just seeing it made me blush with embarrassment again.

"What for?" I exploded. "That's all over and done with."

"Not yet," she said. "Not till after the county spell-down this Saturday. *You'll* have to represent our room now."

"No!" I cried. "I can't!"

"Why not?" she asked.

"Because I'd just make another dumb mistake and embarrass everyone. E-M-B-A-R-R-A-S-*S*."

"Come, come now, Dora," Miss Foster said. "Omitting one letter of one word surely isn't a matter of life and death."

"But my other mistake was," I said.

"What?"

"My other mistake was surely a matter of life and d-d—" I didn't even want to say the word.

"What *are* you talking about?" Miss Foster asked, sounding thoroughly confused.

I explained why I felt responsible that Cora Beth died.

"No, no, no, Dora. You mustn't blame yourself. You were just showing concern for your friend's wishes. She asked you not to tell and you didn't."

"But I had a feeling that I should," I said.

"That may be, but even if you had told me sooner, I'd have done the very same stupid thing. And earlier in the day the stove lid would have been even hotter. It wasn't *your* fault. It was *mine*. I'm the one that put the *heat*"—Miss Foster choked on the word—"on her stomach."

"But you didn't know," I began.

"No." She sighed. "I didn't."

"Papa said it wasn't your fault," I told her.

"He did?" Miss Foster sounded surprised but pleased. "Really?" She wiped at a tear with her handkerchief.

"Really," I assured her. "He said how were you supposed to know; you'd never had any experience with appendicitis."

Almost to herself she said, "No, I hadn't. How nice to know that someone understands that." For the first time since Cora Beth died, I saw the teacher smile a little.

"Papa says it wasn't anyone's fault."

"Not yours, not mine," Miss Foster said. "Let's accept that as the truth, shall we? And get on with what we have to do."

She took a deep, deep breath and stood up extra

straight, like a weight had been lifted off her back. "Now let's review the spelling words." Her voice was getting happy and light again—like the old days.

I shook my head. "I can't do it," I said. "Not now. Not with Cora Beth gone."

"Of course you can," she encouraged. "You need to. In memory of your friend. As a tribute to her."

"If I lose," I said, "it won't be any tribute."

"You won't lose," she insisted. "I *know* you won't."

If she had that much confidence in me, how could I refuse? "All right," I said finally, "I'll do it. For Cora Beth. But will you help me?"

Miss Foster nodded. "For Cora Beth—and *you.*"

That made me feel tingly all over. But I knew that I needed more help than Miss Foster could give. I decided to pray about it.

One thing I never asked for in my prayers was to *win* in a game or a contest. I thought that was playing a dirty trick on God because if everyone prayed to win how could he decide which prayer to answer? This time, though, I did. I prayed to *win*. Not for me, but for Cora Beth.

Every day that week, after school, I reviewed with Miss Foster. At home, I bounced Irene on my knee and sang the letters of the words to her. Making a tune with them helped me to remember. It kept my courage up, too.

Finally the day for the contest arrived. The good-luck heart Cora Beth made for me hung from a ribbon around my neck, out of sight under my dress.

My whole family, wearing their Sunday clothes, rode in the wagon all the way to Portales, more than twenty miles away. When we got there, Miss Foster was waiting at the door. Wordlessly, she pointed to the second row, where all the Tracys were sitting in the audience. I couldn't believe it. Six-month-old Jimmie Joe bounced on his father's knee.

"How could they stand to come?" I whispered to Mama.

"How could they stand not to?" she asked. "You're the only daughter they have left. Today you must carry on for Cora Beth." I must have started to tremble, because Mama grabbed me hard and whispered, "Take a deep breath and calm down. You can do it!"

Miss Foster led me to where I was supposed to sit and gently pushed me into a chair. I didn't look at anyone else. It was as if the other participants weren't even there. As if *I* weren't there.

I scarcely noticed when the contest began. When I stood up to spell, I took that deep breath Mama advised, closed my eyes, and pretended I was Cora Beth. I knew that *she* wouldn't miss, so I imagined that she was the one talking instead of me. The voice that came out of my mouth didn't even sound like mine.

Slowly, carefully, when my turn came, I named the letters in the correct sequence. I capitalized the capitals and remembered the rules about *i* before *e*. I knew when a consonant should be double and when it shouldn't.

After I spelled *accomplishment,* it was all over. Someone handed me a blue ribbon and everyone clapped—Miss Foster hardest of all. Tears of happiness ran down her cheeks, and she held out her arms to me. I hesitated just a second to look up and whisper, "Thank you, God." Then I moved toward my teacher with brimming eyes. The Tracys came up to hug me, and all my family, and someone took a picture for the newspaper.

Now there was just one more thing I had to do. The next morning, as soon as the sun was up, I took the blue ribbon over to the cemetery and left it on Cora Beth's grave. I weighed it down with a pint jar of forget-me-nots.

It almost seemed as if my sister had been with me all during the spell-down. Then she was gone again. I missed her more than ever. When I went back to school on Monday, nothing was the same.

I couldn't decide what to do at recess. The other girls treated me as if I had a deadly disease that they might catch if they came too close. If they did speak to me, they were careful not to mention Cora Beth's name. I wanted to talk about my friend but I could tell that it made everyone else uneasy.

After a while, I figured out that probably no one knew what to say to the best friend of a girl who was dead. At last I understood what Mama had meant when she told me that what you said didn't matter. Showing you cared was the important thing. Ed made his concern clear by inviting me to play marbles with the boys. Caroline walked to school with me instead of hurrying ahead like she usually did.

Cora Beth's empty seat seemed to make a much bigger hole in the schoolroom than the actual space it took up. I was finally reading with the fourth grade group, but that was a hollow victory. I'd lost my desire to skip into fifth grade. If Cora Beth wasn't going to be there next year, I didn't want to be, either. I still stayed after school, but only from habit. Miss Foster tried to excite me about getting ahead again, but I didn't want to try anymore.

I missed going over to the Tracys' to see darling Jimmie Joe, but I couldn't stand to do it with my friend gone. I told myself that having me there would only make Mrs. Tracy feel worse than she already did.

At home, everywhere I looked I saw something that made me remember Cora Beth. Mama did all she could think of to keep me cheered up, but it wasn't any use. The silliest little things made me cry.

One day, with her eyes wet and shining, she said, "Oh, Dora! I wish I could do your grieving for you. But it's something you have to do for yourself. When you lose a loved one, it seems like you have to pay a certain price of pain before you can have peace again. Every person has to do it in his own way and in his own time. It hurts me to see you so sad, but I don't know how to take your sorrow away."

I tried to make a quilt block about Cora Beth, but I couldn't seem to remember anything about our good times together. I knew I had to use a blue block because blue is a sad color. And because of the horrid blue roses. And the forget-me-nots.

I finally decided to appliqué a dirt-colored mound with a heart-shaped wreath of flowers. I embroidered a white bow on it, too. That made it seem like I was tying up my love in a neat little package. I felt better when it was done.

11

Cozy as a Cloud

I continued to hug Henrietta for comfort when I went to sleep. Otherwise, I didn't play with her much. It was too lonely without Cora Beth. I played with a real live doll instead—Irene. Ed spent more time paying attention to me. Even Caroline was extra nice.

I couldn't get the idea of Cora Beth's soft satin bed out of my head. I wanted to make one for Henrietta, fluffy and quilted and cozy as a cloud. I was sure I could find some white flannel scraps in the ragbag. They wouldn't be as elegant as satin but they would be soft. All the flannel had disappeared, though, so I asked Mama what had happened to it.

"I made bibs and washcloths for the baby," she said. "Why don't you use that nice beige cashmere in the bag with the wool pieces?"

"It's the wrong color," I told her.

"I think it's a nice color," she said. "It won't show the dirt."

"Henrietta's bed isn't going to get dirty," I objected.

"Everything gets dirty"—Mama sighed—"with all the dust around here. You know how it is in a windstorm."

Yes, I knew. Sand blasted against the windowpanes and sifted through the window frames. It swirled in eddies against the door. It blew under and over the door and through the tiny cracks. Everything was gritty for days after a windstorm, and just about the time we got all the grime swept and dusted and mopped up, another gale came along and blew it in again. Mama was right, and the beige material *was* very soft. I decided that it would have to do.

I worked for several evenings putting the bed together. First I built a box out of a folded piece of cardboard stitched at the corners. I made the lining exactly the right size to cover the bottom and sides, and glued it on with cooked flour paste. I quilted another piece of material in the same diamond pattern to cover Henrietta. She smiled up at me with her painted eyes wide open as if it felt nice and soft and cuddly.

Caroline decided that she'd like to have a bed for her doll, too. She didn't like to play with dolls much, so I wasn't sure if she really *wanted* one or if she was just trying to be nice to me on account of Cora Beth. She couldn't sew much, herself, so I made another bed and quilt for Lucinda.

Every week, we followed our regular routine of driving ten miles to Clovis for Sunday School in the morning and Meeting in the afternoon. In between, we had dinner with the Lenstroms. Mama always fixed something special to help out with the meal, and Caroline and I enjoyed spending time with Sarah and Jenny. We planned to take our dolls in their new beds the next time we went.

Clovis was the only place that didn't have reminders of Cora Beth. We'd never attended Sunday services together, and she hadn't ever met the Lenstrom girls. Each week, she went to her church and I went to mine. Religion gave me what little comfort I had these days, but soon I was robbed of that, too. Snooty Sister Simpson started all the trouble with her big mouth—on Easter Sunday.

On that day, we didn't take our dolls in their beds, after all. Irene was catching a cold, so Caroline stayed home with her. The rest of us planned to return home right after Sunday School.

"We'll just have to miss the afternoon meeting," Mama told Papa.

"And dinner, too?" Papa asked her.

"With the Lenstroms, yes," she said. "But we'll have a good meal when we get home."

When we arrived at the church, I noticed that most of the ladies and girls had new Easter clothes. Even some of the little children wore hats and gloves. Those who didn't at least had fresh hair ribbons or sashes. Until I saw all that finery, I'd completely forgotten it was Easter.

We Cooksons each wore the same nice clothes Mama had made after Christmas. Ed's outgrown Sunday suit had been handed down to Frank, so he wore his overalls. Mama felt bad about that, but Ed said he didn't care.

"As long as they are clean and mended," Papa assured us, "the Lord won't mind, either." But Sister Simpson surely did. She was dressed fit to kill in a stylish outfit that looked like one of Mandell Clothing's ads in the newspaper. She wore a hat with a bent-back brim, and her snobbish nose was turned up to match.

As soon as we walked in, Sister Simpson tipped her sharp beak down at Mama and snapped, "Well, Betty, it doesn't look like Albert's doing too well on that homestead farm of yours. Can't even afford to buy you something new for Easter."

Mama didn't say anything, but I saw her lip tremble and her whole body sagged like a tomato vine with the wilt. She didn't start to cry, though, until after we got home. As soon as we walked into the house, without speaking a word, she took Irene from Caroline and went into the bedroom to nurse her.

When I followed, a few minutes later, to ask if I should peel some potatoes for dinner, big tears were running silently down Mama's cheeks. I sat on the bed beside her, leaned against her shoulder, and whispered in her ear, "Don't cry, Mama."

"Oh, Dora"—she sobbed—"how I miss Utah! There were always plenty of old suits to make over for the boys, plenty of Cousin Mandy's outgrown frocks to cut down for you and Caroline. We didn't have much money but we could always squeeze out enough to buy Sunday shoes. Remember how you *always* had a new dress for Easter?"

I nodded.

"And a hat?"

"Yes, that you'd made to match my dress."

Then Mama's shoulders stiffened and her voice became angry.

"It's bad enough to have that nosey busybody *Miss* Matilda Simpson put on airs about how grand she is. But when she criticizes your papa as if he couldn't support his family, as hard as he works, that is the last straw! I can tell you, she won't get another chance to do it! *Never, as long as she lives, will I set foot in that church again!*"

It took a lot to get Mama riled, but once she was, watch out. She wiped the tears away impatiently with the back of her hand. "And don't let on that I've been bawling. I wouldn't want Papa to get the notion that I don't appreciate all he does for us."

When Mama told Papa what she'd decided and explained the reason, he just nodded his head as if whatever she wanted to do was okay with him. He always backed Mama up. I could tell that he expected her to change her mind, though.

Every Saturday he asked her if she wanted to go to church the next day.

At first she answered with an emphatic "No!" But before long, she said, "Not yet."

I needed to go—just to get away. I didn't want to wait until Mama was ready, but I didn't have a choice.

When I went to Texico with Mama one Saturday in May, we saw Sister Williamson and Lucy at the store. "Haven't seen you at church for three or four weeks," Sister Williamson said. "Is someone sick?"

"No. No one's sick." Mama's voice made it clear that she didn't intend to say any more to explain her absence.

"What about the girls?" Sister Williamson asked. "Could they go?"

Mama didn't answer right away.

"Say yes, Mama," I begged. "*Please* say yes."

"Please," Lucy added.

"Well, I guess you can go, if you want to," she said.

"I *do* want to," I replied, "and I know Caroline does, too."

"Very well," Mama agreed.

"We'll come by in the morning to get them," Sister Williamson promised, and headed out the door.

Mama suddenly decided that we were going to buy two new hair ribbons instead of the bias tape she needed to finish the apron she was making. We picked out a blue one for me and a red one for my sister.

The next day, Caroline and I were dressed in our Sunday clothes with the new bows in our hair long before it was time to go.

"Why don't you play with your dolls until the Williamsons come by?" Mama suggested.

We went out to the apple orchard, where we'd fixed a playhouse. When we planted the new trees last spring, Papa bought one for each of us children.

"You'll have your own tree to take care of," he said, "and when the fruit is ripe, you can share it with everyone else."

I asked for an orange tree. I'd wanted one ever since I'd first tasted the delicious fruit on Christmas morning. The clerk at the farm supply store just laughed at my request.

"Oranges don't grow here," he told me. "It's too

cold. You need to live in Florida or California to grow oranges."

I settled for an Early Harvest apple tree, and each of the other children had a different variety. Papa dug the holes to plant them twenty feet apart.

"That looks like a long space," I said.

"Not too far for trees that will be fifteen feet across when they are grown," he explained. "Besides, we need to get the cultivating equipment between them to keep the weeds down. We'll plant vegetables between the trees while they grow."

The weeds were already getting pretty thick. Caroline and I had hoed them up near my Early Harvest tree and raked the sandy soil into ridges to outline the rooms of our playhouse. I put Henrietta and Lucinda in the bedroom in their soft beds, and Caroline fixed an imaginary dinner in the pretend kitchen.

Pretty soon the boys came by to see what we were playing. "Looks like your dolls are all ready for their funerals," Ed said.

"They're not dead," I objected, "they're asleep."

"With their eyes open?" George asked.

"We're pretending," I reminded him.

"In their coffins?" Frank asked.

"Those are beds, silly," Caroline explained.

"Look like coffins to me," Frank insisted.

"We could pretend they're dead," Ed said, "and have a funeral."

"Yeah," Frank agreed. "Let's play funeral!"

"Can I be a parlor bearer?" George asked.

"Pallbearer," Caroline corrected.

"Here's a good place for the cemetery," Frank said. "I'll dig the graves."

"You can't bury my doll!" I yelled, panicked at the thought.

"It won't hurt," Ed assured me. "I'll dig her right up again as soon as we're done. I promise."

"You can bury Lucinda," Caroline said. "I don't care."

"You can't bury Henrietta!" I screamed, picking up my doll, bed and all, and hugging her to my chest. No one paid any attention to me.

Frank dug two graves by the Yellow Transparent tree, and Ed found two boards for headstones. He scratched "HENRY ETTA" on one and "LUCINDA" on the other.

"You are not burying Henrietta," I yelled again. "And her name is spelled H-E-N-R-I-E-T-T-A."

"Use your imagination to pretend that I spelled it right," Ed said. "This is only a make-believe funeral, anyway. Remember?"

George stomped down the weeds to make the outline of a church close to his Alexander apple tree.

"We need a place to walk down the aisle," Frank told him, so George smoothed a strip in the middle.

Caroline moved her doll from the bedroom of the house to the living room.

"So everyone can walk by and look at her," she explained.

After the procession walked past the casket, Caroline pulled the quilt over her doll's face to indicate she was dead, and Frank solemnly carried the box with Lucinda in it to the church. Ed preached a short sermon that ended with "ashes to ashes and dust to dust." Then he said, "This coffin needs a lid. Frank, go get a piece of cardboard and some string."

When Frank returned, Ed bent the cardboard over the top of the bed and tied it down—both ways.

"These square knots will never come undone," he assured Caroline as he placed Lucinda's casket in one of the graves.

I didn't like this game at all and hugged my doll even closer. I surely was glad that Henrietta wasn't going to be buried down in that brown hole, especially with eyes that couldn't shut. When the cinnamon-colored soil began covering the top of the cardboard coffin, I felt awful. I was glad, though, that I'd used the beige material to line it with, because the dirt wouldn't show so much if some leaked into the box.

Frank and Ed rounded up the top of the grave and

placed the marker while George ran off to get some cornstalks to make a fence around the cemetery.

"We need some flowers," Caroline said.

I didn't want her putting forget-me-nots on Lucinda's grave. Just the name made the occasion seem too sad—like a real, good-bye-forever funeral.

"I'll get some pansies," I said. "They're blooming by the porch."

Then I did something stupid. I set my doll down so I could hurry faster and headed for the back door.

"I'll go, too," Caroline said, following me.

At exactly that moment, the Williamsons pulled up to take us to Sunday School.

"Hurry, girls," Mama called. "You're almost late."

"Wait till I get my doll," I said, turning back, but Caroline grabbed my hand and jerked me toward the wagon.

"There's no time," she insisted. "Ed will take care of it."

"Ed," I yelled, "bring my doll in." I didn't know if he heard me or not.

All the way to church, Lucy jabbered so much about the Williamsons' new colt that nobody noticed how quiet I was.

I might just as well have stayed at home for all the good it did me to be in Sunday School. I didn't think about Jesus or God or the Ten Commandments or the

Golden Rule or even the Articles of Faith. I didn't hear a thing the teacher said. I worried the whole time about Henrietta. I kept telling myself that she would be all right, that Ed would take her into the house while I was gone, or I could do it myself as soon as I got home.

I couldn't forget that there was still an open grave near our playhouse in the orchard exactly the right size for her cozy bed—and four little brothers who liked to play funeral.

12

Gift from God

The Williamsons stayed after Sunday School to visit their church friends and then stopped at the Lenstroms' on the way back to pick up a harness for their horse. I was so worried about Henrietta that I didn't even enjoy visiting with Jenny Lenstrom. I didn't mention my doll to anyone.

When we finally arrived home, I jumped down from the wagon and ran out to the orchard without even saying thank-you to the Williamsons.

I couldn't believe what I saw. Papa had plowed up the whole field. Not only plowed but disked. Those sharp metal circles had sliced through the weeds over and over again until not a sign of them remained. The sandy soil was as clean and smooth as a sheet of gingerbread. There was no sign of our playhouse. No church. No cemetery. The cornstalk fence was gone, and so were the grave markers.

Surely, Ed must have dug up Lucinda and taken her and Henrietta into the house. That's what I told myself. But I didn't believe it. I had the awful feeling that he hadn't.

"Ed!" I screamed. "Frank!" I ran to find them. They were playing checkers on the front porch.

"What's the matter?" Ed wanted to know.

"Where's my doll?" I asked, trembling.

"Buried in the cemetery," he said, "last time I saw it."

"You buried her?"

"Sure, you left her sitting right next to the grave. I figured you'd changed your mind."

"Didn't you dig her up?" I yelled.

"Nope," he said. "Why should I?"

"Because you *promised* you would!" I shouted.

"All right," he said. "I will. I'll do it as soon as we finish this game."

I choked. "Do it now! *If* you can find her."

"What do you mean, *if* I can find her? She didn't walk away, did she?"

"Come and see for yourself," I answered in an icy voice. "And bring a shovel."

I got one, too, and we went to the orchard together.

"Oh, my gosh!" he said. "What happened?"

"Looks like the ground's been cultivated," I said. I

kept thinking about the sharp plates of the disk going around and around, cutting the weeds to shreds. I didn't want to think about what they might have done to Henrietta. I started to cry.

"Quit bawling!" Ed said. "We'll find your dumb doll."

I knew we wouldn't. And we didn't. We dug for a long time before Papa came looking for us. I was too upset by then to say anything, so Ed told him what had happened.

"Oh, Dora," he said, "I'm so sorry. I had no idea your dolls were out here." Then he began to scold himself.

"I knew I shouldn't be working on Sunday," he said. "There wasn't any emergency. But the ground was perfect for disking and it's time to get the garden in. Thought I'd just get a little head start on Monday and be all ready to put the seeds in first thing in the morning. This should teach me a lesson."

I was surprised that even Papa needed to be taught a lesson.

"That's the last time anyone in this family misses church without a darn good reason," he announced in a determined voice.

He took the shovel from me and began to dig. Papa could do it a lot faster than either Ed or I. He spaded all around the Alexander tree where the cemetery had been, then in wider and wider circles. He uncovered a few scraps of cardboard and some shredded beige cashmere but that was all.

Just before Caroline came to call us to dinner, Papa dug up one of Lucinda's leather arms. It had been sliced in several places by the sharp edges of the disk. When Caroline heard what had happened she said, "Pooh, I don't care. I'm too old to play with dolls anyway."

"I'm not!" I cried. "I'll *never* be too old. I want Henrietta!"

"We'll find her," Papa promised.

"And I don't want her to be all in pieces!" I shouted.

"I can't guarantee that," Papa said. "Maybe we can mend her and maybe we can't."

After dinner Papa and Ed dug until dark. They never found a sign of Henrietta.

Cora Beth and her doll, Rose Marie, were gone. Now Henrietta was gone. I was the only one left of the four of us who used to play house together.

I sat through school the next day in a blue funk, not paying attention to anything that was going on. After everyone else went home, Miss Foster asked, "Would you like to tell me what's been bothering you all day?"

I started to cry and told her about my doll and her bed and the funeral and the plowed field.

"Oh, Dora, I'm sorry," she said. "What a dreadful

thing to happen to Henrietta! I'll bet you felt even worse because it occurred so soon after Cora Beth's death. It must seem like everything bad is piling up all at once."

I nodded.

"Well, we'll just have to change that."

"How?"

"I'm not sure, exactly. But the first thing we have to do is get your brain so busy that there's no time left to feel sorry for yourself."

"How?"

Miss Foster laughed a little. "I *do* know how to do that. I've tried it before. After my mother died, I learned that memorizing poetry took enough concentration to keep me from thinking about how miserable I was. Sometimes, when you're in a black mood, it is good to work on a melancholy piece. It often makes you feel better just to find out that someone else has problems much worse than yours. Even if that doesn't work, you can at least recite the poem in such a somber tone that it puts your audience into a mournful mood, too."

"Why would you want to make them sad?"

"It's part of training your voice to be expressive. All great elocutionists want to make people cry as well as to laugh."

"Well, I don't. And I don't want to be a great anything,

especially a great elo—whatever you said."

"Elocutionist," she repeated.

"I don't even know what that means."

"It means a public speaker who is skilled in making the voice musical and expressive and in using gestures to the best advantage to tell a story to an audience."

"How can you expect me to recite?" I asked. "I've just been talking for a year."

"That's true," Miss Foster said. "You talk so well, I'd forgotten that. It is a big leap for you to recite, but I'm sure you can do it. You'll have to if you want to finish fourth grade."

"I don't want to finish fourth grade."

"Of course you do," Miss Foster insisted, refusing to take me seriously. "I think we'll start with *The Wreck of the Hesperus.* That ought to be sad enough. I've chosen a difficult piece on purpose. Let's read it together so I can help you with the hard words. See if you'd like to trade places with the captain's daughter."

No! I didn't want to trade places with the captain's dead daughter who was "Lashed close to the drifting mast" with "The salt sea . . . frozen on her breast" and "The salt tears in her eyes." I'd rather be just plain Dora Cookson with my own set of problems.

Even the difficult memorization of the grim poem couldn't make me stop missing Cora Beth and Henrietta. Mama said she'd make me a rag doll, but I refused her offer. "I want one like Henrietta," I insisted. No other doll could take Henrietta's place, but I needed a new one to cuddle. And I wanted it to be a twin to the one I lost.

"Well, there's no money to buy one." Mama sighed. "I don't know how you'll get it."

When she said that, I *knew* how I would. I'd ask God.

The privy didn't seem like a very nice place to say a prayer, but with a family the size of ours, the outhouse was the only place to be private. It had a lock on the door. It would have to do.

I sat down on the lid that covered the hole and poured out my heart's desire to God. I spoke softly in case someone might be listening outside and think that I'd gone cuckoo and was talking to myself. I told God how much I missed Henrietta and that I didn't think it was fair that I should be punished because Papa broke the Sabbath. After all, I was at Sunday School, where I should have been, going about the Lord's business. Well, not exactly.

I wasn't really paying much attention to his business that day because I was worrying so much about Henrietta.

I said I didn't know how I could get another doll and that Mama didn't know but I knew that *he* knew, and if he'd just take care of getting me one, I'd be mighty obliged. After praying, I was confident that somehow I was going to have a new doll. I had stayed quite awhile in the privy, wondering how God might answer my prayer, when a hard knock hit the door and Caroline yelled, "I need to come in!"

I unlocked the door and moved out of her way, still wondering.

When I was younger, I would have expected to find the doll in a basket on the doorstep, or sleeping in a rock-a-bye-baby cradle hanging in a tree. I'd figure that maybe God would just drop it down out of the sky. Or send it with a stork the way babies were supposed to be delivered. I'd have looked behind bushes, inside empty boxes, under my pillow.

But I was too old, now, for that kind of nonsense. I had learned that God doesn't do things that way. He uses people to help him answer prayers. I tried to figure out who it would be this time. Miss Foster? Mrs. Tracy? Sister Lenstrom? I waited a week, but nothing happened.

One evening, when the family was sitting at the supper table, someone knocked on the front door. "Go answer it, Dora," Mama instructed. I did, and a big, redheaded, freckle-faced man was standing outside. I wondered if maybe this stranger had come to deliver my doll, but he just stood there, nervously twisting his hat in his hands.

"Is the doctor here?" he asked.

"Nope," I said. "Nobody's sick."

"Isn't this the Cooksons'?"

"Yup."

"Well, Mrs. Owens told me—"

"Oh, you must mean Papa. He's not a real doctor, but sometimes . . ."

"Dora, who is it?" Papa called from the kitchen.

"Someone wants to see you," I called back.

"Bring him on in," Papa said, and stood up as we came through the door. "Evenin'," he said to the man. "What can I do for you?"

"My wife's real bad and I can't find Dr. Wilkins anywhere. Mrs. Owens said you'd saved her baby and I was wonderin' . . ."

"Come on, Betty," Papa said to Mama as he reached for his hat. "I might need your help."

While Mama took off her apron, she instructed Caroline and me to do the dishes and get the children into bed. Then she followed the men out the door.

Back on the night Elizabeth Anne was born to Sister Owens in their covered wagon on the journey from Utah, I didn't know anything about how babies got here. I wasn't any wiser last year on Valentine's Day, when Irene became the baby of our family. But I had learned a few things since then.

Caroline had told me that babies grew inside their mothers' stomachs until they were big enough to be born. I could guess how they got out because our cat had had plenty of kittens and sometimes I'd watched. But I hadn't figured out how babies got inside in the first place. I wasn't about to ask that question again. I'd already tried it. Twice.

Mama told me, "That's something we don't talk about."

And Papa said, "You'll find out when you need to know."

But the night my parents went off with the red-headed man, Papa told me something after they came home that surely surprised me.

Caroline had gone to bed to read as soon as everyone else was tucked in. I was working on a quilt block in the kitchen while I waited for Mama and Papa to come home. I appliquéd a rectangle of brown cloth for the board with Henrietta's name stitched on it—spelled correctly this time. I chose a green square because the orchard was green with weeds the day she was buried.

Papa and Mama finally got back a long time after they left. Mama hurried through the house to make sure everyone was safely asleep, but Papa sat down beside me to talk.

"Did the baby get born yet?" I asked.

"Yup," Papa said. "A fine big boy with red hair. Looks just like his dad." He paused a moment before he added, "The mama's going to be all right, too. For a while it was touch and go."

"How come?" I asked.

"The baby was coming out backward," he explained. "I had to reach in and turn him around so he could squeeze out the right way."

"What if you hadn't?"

"We couldn't have saved him," Papa said. "Might have lost the mother, too."

"How'd you know what to do?" I wanted to know.

"I learned that trick when you were born, Dora," Papa told me. "You wanted to back into the world, too. I was real worried about your mama and praying hard for God to help her bear the pain. Then, all of a sudden, I got this inspiration telling me what I needed to do. It was a miracle that you lived. That's why we called you Dora, because the name means 'gift.' You were a gift from God."

Papa walked with me to the barn and hugged me tighter and longer than usual before he kissed me good-night and waited at the bottom of the ladder while I climbed up to the loft.

After he returned to the house, I lay awake for a long time thinking about what he had said. I was glad he'd learned to turn a baby around in time to save me. If he hadn't, I might be just as dead as Cora Beth Tracy. Mama might be dead, too. That must have been one of the times she felt like she might die.

I was lucky to be alive! Maybe my life had been saved for some special reason. I should quit moping around for my lost friend and wishing for a new doll to play with. It was time I got on with important things. Even if I didn't *want* to skip into fifth grade anymore, I was going to do it anyway. The school year would soon be over, and I had lots of odds and ends to finish if I wanted to catch up to my grade. Would time run out before I completed them?

13

Skip into Fifth

*Miss Foster was glad to hear that I was ready to con-*centrate seriously on my lessons again. "We've lost valuable time," she reminded me, "and there's still a great deal to do. You're not even halfway through the fourth reader; there are five or six more poems to memorize; your geography maps are"—she shook her head in despair—"not what they should be."

Each thing she mentioned felt like another ten pounds heaped on my shoulders. Then she laid on the backbreaking straw: "And I haven't said anything to Mr. Stern about our plan yet. I don't know if he'll approve or not." My face must have shown that I felt the whole project sounded impossible.

Miss Foster warmed me with her brightest smile and said cheerfully, "But I think we can do it. Don't forget that you have all day every day during school—plus an extra hour of private tutoring. You'll be surprised how many short snatches of time you can find to study when you start looking for them. You already learned to do two things at once by using the poems you needed to memorize for penmanship practice."

I guess I still looked discouraged, because she added emphatically, "No matter what, don't *ever* give up your dream. Only you can make it come true."

That gave me the encouragement I needed. I could learn the poems while I walked home from school or to and from the pasture to get the cow for milking.

I practiced saying my pieces out loud while I tended the baby. Whether Irene could understand all the words or not didn't matter as long as I made my voice go high and low, fast and slow, or gestured to and fro enough. I could entertain her just by the expressions on my face while I talked.

Even though the story was sad, I had learned to love the words and the wonderful rhythm of *The Wreck of the Hesperus*. It was almost like singing a song to say

Blue were her eyes as the fairy-flax,
Her cheeks like the dawn of day,
And her bosom white as the hawthorn buds,
That open in the month of May.

When Mama heard me reciting, she gasped.

"That's no story to be reading to a baby," she objected. "It's too scary. *The Children's Hour* would be more suitable for Irene. Or *Robin Redbreast,* or the one about the seasons by Thomas Bailey Aldrich."

"You mean *Marjorie's Almanac*?"

"Yes, that's the one."

It was fine with me to read the happier poems to Irene. I needed to memorize them, too.

One day after school, Miss Foster was absolutely beaming. "I've finally figured out," she began, "a foolproof map you can draw for your geography project. It's so easy and so timely, I can't imagine why I didn't think of it sooner."

"What?" I asked, doubtful that any map could be easy.

"New Mexico," she said. "Almost every line is straight—all around the outside edge and along the county borders, too. You could do it with a ruler."

That sounded good to me.

"But when you get to the rivers," Miss Foster warned, "please, PLEASE, *don't* use your imagination. Get Ed to help you. He's good with geography, you know. Especially maps."

Although he hated to do homework, Ed sat right by me while we measured out the square lines of New Mexico on one map and drew them on another.

There were jigs and jags in some of the county lines, but almost all of them were straight.

"There are only three states easier to draw than ours," Ed told me. "Wyoming, Colorado, and Utah. And I'll bet their county lines are crooked. I wouldn't be surprised if New Mexico has more straight lines than any state in the U.S.A.!"

"Let's just call it the Straight State, then," I suggested as I continued to measure and draw. Finally, I had finished the last county line.

"What are all those marks that look like pointy peaks?" I asked Ed.

"Mountains," he replied.

"Mountains?" I questioned. "In New Mexico? This state is as flat as a pancake."

"This *part* of the state—the great plains—is flat," Ed told me. "There are lots of mountains in the north and west."

"That's news to me," I said, and copied a few on my map. "Now that I'm done with the straight lines, you can draw the wiggly rivers."

"I can't do that on *your* map," Ed objected. "That would be cheating."

"Miss Foster said you could."

"She said I could *help*. And the best way to help is to teach you how to do it yourself." I'd heard that before. Papa said it all the time.

"I can't do it," I wailed. "I've tried a thousand times."

"You just don't know the secret," Ed said. "First you have to *look* at the rivers—really study them. Where do they start? Where do they end? Which direction do they go?"

The Rio Grande cut a north/south slash right through the state from Colorado to Mexico. The Pecos River ran almost as far in the same direction but farther east. I remembered following it when we moved from Utah. The San Juan dipped down in a half circle by the Four Corners area, and the Canadian carved out a squarish section in the northeast corner.

"Now what?" I asked after I'd studied awhile.

"Start with the shortest—the San Juan. You've already done part of it. It's that crooked corner of San Juan County. The secret to copying is to follow the original line with your eye while the pencil is drawing it on the other paper. Don't watch where you are writing."

"That doesn't make any sense," I objected. "You *have* to watch the pencil."

"No, you don't. I'll show you." Ed picked up a clean piece of paper to demonstrate. While looking just at the map, he drew the Rio Grande. I couldn't believe how much the line looked like the one he was copying. "Try it," he said, handing me the pencil.

My results were not as good as Ed's, and I hesitated at doing a long river.

"Do it county by county," he suggested. "It's always smart to break a big job into smaller parts." For a boy who hated school, Ed was no dummy.

I worked on the rivers county by county until the map was done. Miss Foster was pleased and put it in a folder with my best penmanship papers.

I decided to put the map of New Mexico on my next quilt block to remember all the lessons we'd had about our new state. I'd make a yellow shape on a red square with blue rivers, brown mountains, and red names, but not until after school was out. I'd have more time then.

I practiced "dip, drip, write" so much that the refrain just went on automatically in my head every time I picked up a pen. My writing was much improved since I had copied all the poems. One afternoon during my private session with Miss Foster, I was doing *The Village Blacksmith* in my best handwriting. She tiptoed quietly behind me so she wouldn't disturb me while she checked on my progress.

"Very nice," she whispered, and continued out the door and around the building to Mr. Stern's room. She had mentioned that she was going to talk to him about the possibility of moving me up some extra grades. I went on with the writing:

And children coming home from school,
Look in at the open door;

They love to see the flaming forge,
And hear the bellows roar,
And catch the burning . . .

I was just reaching up to dot the *i* in *burning* when I heard a bellowing roar from the other side of the drop-down door. The sudden sound startled me so much that I jumped, jiggled the pen, and dropped a messy blot on my almost-perfect paper.

"Ab-so-lutely not!" Mr. Stern thundered.

That's all I heard except for Miss Foster's muffled voice and the principal's gruff replies. But those two words were enough to give me the message. They were just as fast and final as the thunk of an axe killing a chicken. In that short second, my page was ruined, my hopes were shattered, my dream was dead.

I crumpled the paper, dropped it in the wastebasket, and left the room without waiting for Miss Foster to return. I didn't want to talk to her about what had just happened.

She didn't say anything about it, either, when she saw me the next day. We both acted the same as usual. I knew I had to finish out the last week of school no matter how hopeless I felt, so I completed the *Riverside Fourth Reader*, handed in some pretty good penmanship papers, and recited my memorized poems to Miss Foster.

I was also practicing different gestures, facial expressions, and voice variations for my recitation of *The Wreck of the Hesperus* on the final day of school. All the fourth graders had to say a piece. Ever since the county spell-down in Portales, I was not afraid of reciting in front of the class. I'd found out that I could temporarily become a different person while I did it. Also, I could concentrate hard enough not to let other things bother me. That's what I *thought*, anyway. Mr. Stern gave my theory the true test.

Miss Foster had warned me that she was going to invite him in to listen, but when he was not there when we began, I decided he wasn't coming. Miss Foster was standing in the back of the room by the door, and as soon as I had announced my poem, I saw her leave.

A moment later, she returned with Mr. Stern and my heart began to pound in double time. Would I panic? Make a mess of things? No! I'd do what I'd prepared to do to the best of my ability. I'd make my teacher proud of me, not ashamed.

My voice and my expressions made the storm so fearful and the wreck so real and the cold so frigid that my classmates were shivering in their seats. When I said the part about the salt tears in the frozen daughter's eyes, I had some glistening in mine, too.

Mr. Stern stayed until the last stanza was finished,

nodded briefly, and was gone again. Everyone clapped when I was done and I blushed with pleasure.

"What a fine dramatic rendition!" Miss Foster said, smiling at me as I sat down. "Last year at this time," she told the class, "Dora was just learning to talk after an operation on her tongue. She's come a long way since then, hasn't she?"

Everyone clapped again. I *had* come a long way. But not far enough for Mr. Stern to allow me to skip into his room. I was glad I hadn't mentioned my goal to any of my classmates.

When Miss Foster handed out the report cards that afternoon, she saved mine till the last and dismissed everyone else before she gave it to me.

I saw an *E* for excellent in every subject except geography and that was *G* for good. I turned the page over to see what she'd written where it said "Promoted to Grade _____." There was a question mark in the blank space.

"What does this mean?" I asked.

"It means that I don't know yet," Miss Foster said. "Mr. Stern was somewhat skeptical about having you skip so many grades at once, but I convinced him to consider it." I smiled with pleasure, remembering how persuasive Miss Foster could be with Mr. Stern. "He has agreed to give you a test in the fall to determine which grade you should be in. I think you can do *most* fifth grade work. But some of it might be too hard for you. There are a few more things I wish you knew before you go into Mr. Stern's room."

"I'll learn them!" I insisted.

"I hoped you'd say that." She pointed to three books on her desk. "I have some extra reading for you to do over the summer. I've put a note in the front of each book telling you which parts are especially important to study and another at the back indicating which one to read next." Wasn't that just like Miss Foster—to make a game of it? "But," she warned with a twinkle in her eye, "no fair reading the notes ahead of time!"

"I won't," I promised, scanning the titles. *Fairy Tales* by Hans Christian Andersen, *The Children's Own Longfellow*, and *Anne of Green Gables* by L. M. Montgomery.

"Where do I start?" I asked.

"With the fairy tales," she said. She opened her bottom drawer and handed me a stack of papers. "I saved all the assignments you turned in. Don't get rid of them yet; you may need them later. Do you still have all the notes you took?" I nodded. "Save those, too. Here's some writing paper and an extra pencil in case you need them."

"Where will you be in case I need you?" I asked.

"Too far away to be much help, I'm afraid," Miss

Foster said. "I'm going home to spend the summer with my family in Santa Fe. But I'll be back the week before school starts."

"I'll miss you," I said.

"I'll miss you, too," she replied, holding out her arms for a hug.

I stacked everything in a neat pile so I could carry it all home. I left with a heavy load but a light heart. By fall I'd be ready for that test!

After I got home, I put all the papers away in my treasure chest by my bed. Then I checked the number of pages in each book and added them up: 755. I wanted to divide that number by how many days I had to read them.

"When does school start?" I asked Mama.

"My goodness, Dora," she replied, "summer vacation hasn't even begun and you already want to know when it's going to be over? You take this education business pretty seriously, don't you?"

I showed her the question mark on my report card and told her what it meant. "I need to know how many pages I have to read each day," I told her.

"Well," she said, "I can tell you the exact date school will begin—the day after Labor Day."

"When's that?"

"The first Monday in September." Mama flipped though the pages of the calendar until she found the one she was looking for. "That's September second, this year," she said. "You'd better plan to be done by the first—or even sooner would be better. Don't forget you'll need a few days to review for the test."

I added up the days of June, July, and August plus three days of May. "Ninety-five days," I said, figuring with a pencil, "less five days for review makes . . . 755 pages divided by ninety days. That's 8.38 pages a day. I'll round it off to nine."

"It's a good idea to pace yourself like that," Mama said, "to make sure you get done. But, if I were you, I'd read as much as I could as fast as I could. You never know what may come along to delay you."

14

Swat the Fly

I'd already forgotten how busy we were in the summer. Our farm always required more work than we could possibly do. The vegetable garden was thriving already. It needed to be weeded and thinned. After that was done, we started on the broomcorn. Each stalk had to be circled with a white crayon so the ants wouldn't crawl up and bring the aphids that could suck the life out of the crop.

As a rule, Caroline helped Mama in the house and the boys and I worked with Papa outside. Some projects, however, required the efforts of everyone.

In my spare time, I read as fast as I could in the fairy tale book, listing the titles and themes of each story as Miss Foster's note instructed. I knew that in no time at all we'd begin canning food again for the winter months. There wouldn't be much time for reading then. Most of the fruit jars we'd filled last year were sitting on the cellar shelves with their mouths open, looking hungry.

"I thought we wouldn't have to can so much food in New Mexico," Papa said one pleasant June evening. "I expected fruit and vegetables to grow all year round. But I sure was mistaken about that. It gets colder in the winter than I figured."

"And cooler on summertime nights, too," Mama reminded him.

"Yup," Papa agreed. "This thin, dry air loses heat in a hurry as soon as the sun goes down."

"And heats up even faster the next morning when it rises," Mama said, swinging the flyswatter.

"It's good weather for growing crops, though," Papa said, sitting down to read the weekly newspapers. They had been piling up, waiting for him to get around to them.

"And good weather for growing flies," Mama said, hitting the table with a smack and flicking another dead fly onto the floor. "I've never seen as many as this year."

"Nope," Papa said absently, and kept on reading. All of a sudden, he jumped up and waved the paper. "Whooee!" he shouted. "Listen to this! 'A new homestead law has been approved by Congress. Now only three years' residence is required instead of five.'"

"Really?" Mama asked. "Are you sure?"

"That's what it says, right here in black and white," Papa replied, showing the paper to Mama.

"That's what it says," she repeated. "It's in a letter from our congressman, H. B. Fergusson. We *can* get our title in three years instead of five. Why do you think the government changed the law?" Mama asked.

"So it would be easier for farmers to earn land, I guess," Papa replied.

"Anything else different?" Mama asked.

"Lots," Papa said. "'Five months' absence will be allowed each year; no cultivation required the first year, one sixteenth required the second year, and one eighth the third year.'" He stopped reading and thought quickly. "That means we only have to get ten acres planted this year!"

"We've done that already, haven't we?" Mama asked.

"Yup," Papa agreed. "Everything else we do is getting ahead for next year."

"Well, that sure is good news!" Mama said.

"Does that mean we're halfway up our rainbow?" Caroline asked.

"Up and over the top," Mama said.

"From now on it's downhill all the way," Ed added, remembering what Mama had promised when she hung the picture on the wall.

Now that the homestead law was changed, I had only half as long to finish my rainbow quilt. I'd have to make twice as many blocks each year or else leave every other square plain and arrange them like a checkerboard.

Papa finished one paper and picked up another. After a while, he asked, "Did I hear you complaining about the flies?"

"Yes!" Caroline replied, waving her hand in front of her face. "They're awful."

"Tells here how to get rid of them," Papa said.

"I want to hear that!" Mama said with another slap of her swatter.

"A sale on flypaper?" Caroline asked.

"A giant-size swatter?" I wondered.

"A new kind of fly trap?" Ed guessed.

"Nope," Papa replied, "a swat-the-fly contest. Listen to this: 'A campaign was inaugurated against the housefly, and war has been declared.'"

"Sounds like a good idea," Mama agreed, "but I surely wouldn't want to be the one to win that contest!"

"Why not?" Papa asked.

"It would be like advertising that you had the dirtiest place in town if you could kill the most flies there."

"No, it wouldn't," Papa argued. "It would announce that you had the cleanest because you got rid of the most."

"What's the prize?" Ed wanted to know.

Papa continued reading: "'The Chamber of Commerce is offering one hundred dollars in cash prizes as follows: Any person under eighteen years of age may enter the contest. The person delivering . . . the most dead flies before June twenty-second is to receive a cash prize of seventeen dollars and fifty cents.'"

I could tell by the look on Ed's face that he was already figuring out how he could spend that much money. I knew what I'd buy—my very own dictionary, like Cora Beth's. I knew I'd need one to find out what some of Longfellow's words meant.

Papa went on, "Second prize, twelve dollars and fifty cents; third prize, eight dollars; fourth prize, six dollars; fifth prize, four dollars; sixth prize, five each, three dollars; seventh prize, six each, two dollars; eighth prize, twenty-five each, one dollar—a total of one hundred dollars in forty-one prizes."

Even one dollar sounded like a lot of money to me. I wondered if it would buy a book. All I knew about money was that a penny would buy a stick of candy, a package of dye cost a dime, and Mama could trade a dozen eggs for a little sack of sugar.

Papa kept on reading, "'The slogan of the Chamber of Commerce will be Swat the Fly. By the close of this campaign, we expect to be able to say to the world: There are no flies in Clovis. On with the battle.'"

"Wouldn't that be nice, not to have any more of these pesky things buzzing around," Caroline said, brushing a fly off her face.

"They're more than pesky," Mama said. "They're a downright health hazard."

"That's a fact," Papa agreed, still reading from the newspaper. "Dr. Worley says here that each fly can carry fifteen hundred typhoid germs on each leg. 'He may pass over the table, drop this dreaded germ in our soup, light on our bread and butter, or sup out of the glass with us.'"

"Really, Albert," Mama scolded, slapping the swatter again. "You can omit the gruesome details."

"Just quoting the doc," Papa defended himself.

I wondered how many typhoid germs I'd already swallowed from the flies that swarmed around our table every day.

"San Antonio, Texas," Papa said, "had a fly-swatting contest last year, and typhoid statistics were lower than they've ever been. Listen to this: 'The result was the slaughter of 1,250,000 flies, making a pyramid three feet high and five feet long, and according to government figures destroying destructive germs to the number of more than one trillion. The winner was an eleven-year-old boy who brought in a forty-pound sugar sack containing half a million dead flies.'"

I wondered who had counted all those dead flies. I wasn't even sure I remembered how many zeros one million had, let alone a trillion. I could just imagine Miss Foster making the whole contest into arithmetic problems when school started: "If Jack killed ten flies, how many typhoid germs did he destroy?"

Papa continued, "Dr. Dickman writes that 'flies have killed more people in Clovis alone than have been killed by rattlesnakes in the entire state in the last ten years.'"

While Papa was reading, Ed had already begun to pick up the dead flies Mama had flicked onto the floor. "Here's eleven," he said, dropping them into an empty fruit jar.

"Are you going to enter the contest, Ed?" Papa asked.

"I'm going to *win* it!" Ed announced.

"Well, it tells here how to make the trap used by the winner in Worcester," Papa said.

"Let me see that," Ed said. It was the first time in my life I'd ever seen Ed want to read anything.

While I was helping Ed find the materials to build the fly trap, we talked about his strategy.

"There are two ways to win a contest," he said. "Work harder than anyone else or be smarter. I expect to do both."

"And get more people to help," I said.

"Yeah, and start right now," Ed said.

"And stop at the last minute," I suggested. "Don't take your flies in until June twenty-second. That means we have sixteen days."

I did an arithmetic problem in the dirt: *If Ed swatted half a million flies in sixteen days, how many would he have to kill in one day?*

"You'll have to get over thirty-one thousand flies a day," I told him, "to beat the boy who won in San Antonio."

"Thirty-one thousand!" Ed exclaimed. "I can't even count that far."

"Sure you can," I told him. "It's only one thousand thirty-one times. And"—I did some more figuring—"if everyone in the family helps, that's only two thousand, eight hundred and forty each."

"That's a lot less!" Ed said.

"Yep," I agreed.

"Now," he said, "what we need is nine jam jars."

"Why not a dozen?" I asked, thinking the more the better.

"Because," he said in his don't-be-stupid voice, "we only have nine people in the family." Of course. I should have figured that out.

Ed put the jars in a line on the kitchen windowsill. He wrote our names on scraps of paper, one for each jar: Papa, Mama, Caroline, Dora, Ed, Frank, George, Howard, and Irene.

"Think Irene's big enough to help?" Ed asked.

"Sure," I said. "She loves to pick up flies."

"I'll need you to help me count the dead ones when we've got them all collected," Ed said. "You're good with numbers."

"Yeah," I admitted. "But it will take too long if we wait till then. We should do it every day."

"Okay by me," he agreed.

"Better still," I suggested, "why don't we have each person count their own? I'll help Irene. When we get a hundred flies we can put a mark by our name and dump the flies into a big jar. That way I'll just have to add up the marks and multiply by one hundred."

"Good idea."

"And everyone ought to have his own swatter."

"You're right," he said. "The Chamber of Commerce is giving them out free. I'll ride the horse into town and pick some up."

As soon as Ed came back, he passed out the free flyswatters, explained his plan, and promised a share of the prize money to everyone who helped. Right away, the whole family was like an army swatting and squashing and picking up flies as soon as our daily chores were done.

Then Ed built a large box with four window screens we'd found at the junkyard. He nailed a board across the top and drilled a hole in the center.

"What's that for?" I asked.

"To put this through," he said, picking up a screened, funnel-shaped cage with a small opening at the narrow end. It fit neatly into the hole.

After the trap was assembled, I asked Ed, "Where are you going to put it?"

"Behind the barn," he told me, taking hold of one end of the box and pointing to the other for me to help him move it. "That's the place where the flies are thickest."

We set the trap on small blocks to lift it off the ground.

"Now we need some bait to coax the flies inside," Ed said.

"What kind?" I asked.

"The Worcester boy it told about in the paper used old fish heads," he said.

"Where you gonna get those?"

"Can't," he said. "We'll have to use something else."

"Would chicken heads do?"

"Prob'ly. Or innards."

"Mama'll kill a chicken on Saturday."

"Until then," Ed decided, "I'll just use some manure.

It always draws plenty of flies."

"Honey draws flies, too," I said. "And they stay stuck in that."

"Go get some," he told me. "I'll drizzle it on top of the manure."

Once the trap was in place, the bait underneath was soon swarming and humming with hungry flies.

"Now we need to sew enough gunnysacks together to wrap around the box."

"What for?" I asked.

"To make it dark inside."

"Why?" I needed to know.

"Didn't I tell you how this thing works?"

"Nope," I said. "How does it?"

"I'll show you."

Ed picked up a scrub brush and scratched on the screen. The noise scared the flies off the manure up into the screened box—except for the ones caught in the drizzled-on honey.

"Now, if we cover the lower part of the box," Ed said, "the flies will go up toward the light right into the trap on top."

"How will we swat them there?"

"Won't need to," Ed said. "After dark, when the flies have settled down to sleep, we'll empty the funnel into a quart jar and screw on the lid. The next day we'll put the bottle in the sun and the heat will kill 'em all. After they're dead, we'll count 'em."

"I'll get two needles and some thread," I volunteered, "if you'll find the sacks."

"Okay," Ed agreed.

A few minutes later, while we sat stitching the sacks together, Ed told me what else he had in mind.

15

Hatch More, Catch More

Ed and I finished stitching the gunnysacks together and placed them around the bottom of the fly trap. We watched the flies move into the funnel on top.

"I heard something over in Clovis today that gave me an idea," Ed said.

"What?" I wanted to know.

"That if one pair of houseflies mated in April and all their eggs hatched and lived and laid more eggs, by August the earth would be covered with flies forty-seven feet deep."

"I don't believe it."

"I don't believe it, either," he agreed. "But I started thinking about it. And what I decided is that you could catch more flies if you could hatch more flies."

That made sense to me. "Yeah," I agreed. "But how?"

"You've seen the white maggots on top of the cow pies?"

"Sure."

"And you know they've hatched from fly eggs?"

"Yeah, those little yellow specks that look like tiny snips of thread."

"And you know that the maggots'll turn into flies?"

"Yeah."

"Then why don't we gather up all the cow pies and wait for the flies to hatch?"

"We could," I agreed. "Let's stack them all up and cover the whole pile with mosquito netting to keep the flies inside."

"Good idea," Ed said, heading for the pasture to collect cow pies. Flies were swarming around the gooey fresh splats.

"Probably laying their eggs," Ed said. "Let's look for some with maggots."

We found the squirmy worms on the pies that had dried. They were easier to pick up than the wet ones.

We stacked the stinky circles carefully on top of each other so the wriggly maggots wouldn't drop off, and started back to the barn with our loads piled up like pancakes wedged underneath our chins. I couldn't see where I was going, tripped, and dumped my whole armful.

"Darn you, Dora!" Ed yelled. "Look how many you've wasted."

"Wouldn't be wasted," I said, looking down at the scattered mess, "if we made the pile right here."

"No, I guess not," Ed said. "We might as well do that. Flies can hatch anywhere." Ed set down his armload and spread out the cow pies in an orderly pattern, staggering the second row enough to leave most of the tops exposed.

"Might as well be neat about it," he said, "and leave room for a little air to get through. Flies might need to breathe, the same as we do."

"I'll go get the mosquito netting," I offered.

"Bring the shovel, too," Ed called after me.

We lifted the netting over the top of the stack and shoveled dirt around the edges to keep it anchored down. Our hatchery was in place.

Every day we lifted a corner of the netting and added more maggot-covered cow splats to the pile. We went farther and farther from home to find them. Finally we had a stack half as tall as Ed. It was as many as the netting could cover. Only a few flies buzzed underneath it. Would our maggots hatch in time for the final dead fly count? We could only hope.

Day by day we watched. Not much happened in the fly hatchery except that the squirmy maggots grew fatter and fatter on their diet of manure. So fat, in fact, that they popped right out of their skins and grew some more.

Everyone was swinging and swatting and adding up flies. Frank and George preferred the pig pen; Caroline took Howard out to the chicken coop. Mama let Irene pick up the ones that she swatted in the house. She made sure we all scrubbed our hands before we ate.

I decided to make an *X* on the tally sheet for each thousand as Ed poured them into the flour sack. Then a * for each ten thousand.

"Have you ever noticed," I asked Ed one day, "that after dark you never hear a fly buzzing around outside but that there's always some humming in the house next to the lamp?"

"Sure," he said. "They go for the light."

"Then why don't we take a lamp out to the barn where the flies are the thickest? That way we could swat flies at night as well as in the daytime."

"Yeah," he said. "I'll get that old lamp down in the cellar and fill it with kerosene."

We killed and counted quite a few flies before Papa came out and discovered what we were doing.

"That's a pretty good idea," he said, "but too dangerous."

"Dangerous for the flies, maybe," Ed agreed.

"No," Papa said firmly, "dangerous for you. What do you think would happen if you accidentally knocked the lamp over with all this dry hay around?"

"It'd spill the kerosene," Ed said.

"And set the barn on fire!" Papa said.

"But we won't tip it over," Ed argued. "We're careful. And look how many flies we got already."

"It's too dangerous," Papa repeated, picking up the lamp, "*and I don't want you to try it again!* All the contest prizes in the world aren't worth taking that kind of chance. Besides, it's bedtime."

He told us good-night and not to forget to say our prayers, and took the lamp back into the house. We climbed up the ladder to bed.

The next morning, we went out to the pasture to check our hatchery. I couldn't see any maggots anywhere. Nothing was wriggling on top of the cow pies.

"They're all gone!" I gasped.

"They can't be gone," Ed said, kneeling down. He stared a long time and finally said, "You're right. The maggots are gone."

"But where?" I wanted to know.

"Right inside those hard striped cases that have dropped down on the ground. Those are the things that'll hatch into flies."

"How long will it take?" I asked.

"Don't know," he said. "Not long, I hope. There's only five days left."

We watched and watched. The flies didn't hatch that day. Or the next.

It was getting harder and harder to find flies to swat.

We had killed and counted nearly three hundred thousand and the supply had dwindled to a handful.

I took my book and read while Ed watched the hatchery. I hadn't looked at a book since the contest began. Too bad Miss Foster hadn't told me to study arithmetic. I was having plenty of practice with numbers!

Frank and George went to all the neighbors to ask if they could swat their flies. Ed and I walked over to the Pearces' to see how many Willie had collected. He had a quart jar nearly full.

Ed told him about our collection.

"You got *how many flies*?" Willie exclaimed.

"Nearly three hundred thousand," Ed repeated.

"Then you might as well have mine, too," Willie said. "No use me entering the contest."

"You might win *one* of the prizes," Ed told him.

"But not *first*," I added proudly. "Ed's gonna win first."

"Naw," Willie said. "I don't wanna."

"You sure?"

"Yeah, I'm sure." Willie handed Ed his jar. "Take 'em."

"How many are there?" I asked.

"Dunno," he said. "You'll have to count 'em."

So we did.

On Friday, June 21, our flies started to hatch. The

manure pile under the netting sounded like an angry hive of bees.

"What do we do now?" I asked. "If we take off the net they'll all fly away. If we don't, how can we swat them?"

Ed had already figured that out. He slapped the swatter hard against the netting and some of the flies inside fell dead. Some, though, were only stunned and soon began buzzing again. The live flies were hitting against the net like popcorn trying to get out of a popper.

"We'll kill 'em all," Ed said, "and then we'll count 'em." Both of us swatted until our arms ached.

In the afternoon, Ed sent me to the house to coax Frank and George to come help. Before the day was over, everyone had joined us and nine swatters slapped against the net. Piles of flies lay dead inside. Every time Ed started to take off the net to count them, he'd see another fly moving. "We may just need that one to win," he'd say, and take another swat.

One by one, our helpers went into the house to have supper. I stayed with Ed while he waited and watched. It seemed like the longest day of the year. I guess June 21 always is. Finally the sun went down, the air became chilly, and all sound and movement stopped inside the net. "We'll count them in the morning," Ed said. "It won't take long."

By the time I had eaten and gone to bed, I never

wanted to see another fly as long as I lived. Dead or alive. But the contest wasn't over yet.

At breakfast the next day we made our plans for delivering the flies to the Chamber of Commerce. "What time do they close?" Ed wanted to know.

"Probably six o'clock on a Saturday," Papa said.

"We'll have to go earlier than that," Mama said. "I need to get some things at the store."

"I do, too," Papa said. "Let's all work hard this morning and be ready to leave right after dinner. About two."

"The boys can go with Ed and Dora to count the flies," Mama said, "but Caroline needs to stay here and help me with the Saturday cleaning."

More flies had hatched in the night, and Ed started hitting at the net again. "You've got to stop swatting and start counting!" I insisted. "It's going to take longer than you think."

It did. And it was a mess. The flies were mashed together. Most of the wings were gone. We had to pick them apart, and it took a long time. New ones were still hatching, and Ed tried to swat them all. Each of us had a jar and I kept the tally sheet. Miss Foster would have been proud of me.

At noon Papa came to tell us to come to dinner. He saw the mess we were in and stayed to help. Then Mama came. "Food's getting cold," she said.

"I'm sorry, hon," Papa said. "We can't come now."

"Looks like we've got a long way to go," Mama said, pitching right in to help.

Caroline came next, with Irene, and they stayed, too. The sun got hotter and hotter. Irene lay down on the ground and went to sleep. About four o'clock Papa said, "We'll never make it to Clovis if we don't leave soon. Frank, go get a shovel and some gunnysacks. We'll let the Chamber of Commerce count the rest."

We didn't have time to separate any more dead flies from the mashed-up manure, so we took it all. Bags and bags.

"It won't do any good for me to go to the store this late in the day," Mama told Papa when we finally had the wagon loaded up. "It'll be closed as soon as we get there. Just take Ed and Dora. I'll stay home and get everyone else fed and bathed for Sunday."

There was no time for Papa to argue or for us to get cleaned up. "Hurry," he said. "We'll have to go as we are."

Papa and Ed were filthy and smelly. Dust and sweat ran down their cheeks and mixed in muddy streaks. I must have looked the same.

When we got to the office where the flies were supposed to be delivered, a Closed sign hung in the window. My heart dropped with a thud that made me sick. Was all that work for nothing?

"Oh, no!" Ed choked, and a tear trickled down his cheek. I'd never seen Ed cry before. *"Oh, no!"*

"Don't worry," Papa said. "We'll take them to B. D. Oldham's house."

"Whose?" Ed wanted to know.

"Oldham's," Papa repeated. "He's the president of the Chamber of Commerce. I know where he lives."

"Hurry," Ed said with despair in his voice. "It's probably already too late."

"It is *not* too late," Papa insisted in his nobody-better-argue-with-me voice. "June the twenty-second lasts until midnight, and B. D. Oldham himself is not going to tell me that it's too late. Not until the clock strikes twelve. That's nearly six hours from now."

The house we were looking for wasn't far, but no one was home. "Where's Oldham?" Papa asked a neighbor who was sitting on his front porch.

"Prob'ly still countin' flies," he replied. "He's had a busy day today."

"He's going to be busier," Papa said. "Where can we find him?"

"Moved the collectin' place down behind Steed's Funeral Parlor," he said, "after they ran outa room at the office."

"So the undertaker would be handy for all the dead flies?" Papa joked. "That sounds appropriate." He tipped his hat and clucked "Giddyup" to the horses. "Much obliged," he called as we drove away.

We found five or six men sorting out boxes and bags and bottles of flies. They had barrels and bowls and bins of flies. Jars and jugs and jiggers of flies. Cans and crocks and cruets of flies. But they greeted us with enthusiasm. They were anxious to have even more dead flies than they already had.

Papa and Ed unloaded all the ones we'd counted, and I gave the tally sheet to the man who seemed to be in charge.

"That's a mighty lot of dead flies," he said. "Could be the most."

"We've got more," Ed said.

"Didn't have time to count 'em," Papa apologized. "You'll have to do that, I guess."

"Be glad to," the man said. But he looked as if he'd changed his mind when he saw how many bags we had.

"Some of it's dirt," Papa explained when he plopped the last sack on the ground by the others.

"But most of it's flies," I added.

"Lots and lots of flies," Ed said.

"Yes, I can see that. Sure looks like you're the winner."

Ed held out his hand and asked, "Can I have my money now?"

The man laughed. "No, not yet. Somebody might bring in more flies than you did. I doubt it. But they might. It's still June twenty-second, you know."

Just a short time ago that fact was in our favor. Now it wasn't. We were ready for the contest to be over now, while we were still ahead. Ed wanted to wait until midnight to see what happened.

"Can't stay," Papa told him. "We've got to eat and get cleaned up for church tomorrow. You'll have to wait to find out if you won."

16

Money in the Bank

Ed worried all the way back that someone else might win the contest. "When will I know?" he asked Papa.

"Dunno," Papa told him.

"How will I find out?"

"Dunno," Papa said again. "We shoulda asked."

"You might get a letter," I suggested.

"Probably will," Papa agreed. "You had your name on that list of numbers, didn't you?"

"I *hope* so," Ed said with panic in his voice. "Did we, Dora?"

"Of course," I told him. "I put it right at the top in capital letters."

"They might not announce the winner for a long time," Papa said, "if they have to count all those dead flies again."

"It would be crazy to do that," I said.

Papa laughed. "Sure would, but you never know."

Mama was still keeping supper warm on the back of the stove when we got home. "Did you get there in time?" she asked as she dished up our plates and we scrubbed our hands and faces, one at a time, in the washpan.

"Yup," Papa said, drying his hands on the towel that Mama had made from flour sacks and hung on a roller on the wall.

"Did you win?"

"Don't know yet," Ed said wearily, sinking down on a chair.

"We had the most so far," I added.

"Sounds like a good sign," Mama said.

"Well," Papa said, "whether you won or not, you did your best. That's what counts."

"Getting rid of all those flies counts, too," Mama added. "That counts plenty!"

But Ed didn't hear either one of them. He had both elbows on the table propping up his head. He was sound asleep.

We were all glad that the next day was Sunday. We needed a day of rest. I wanted to lean back in the hayloft after church and read Andersen's *Fairy Tales*. I'd lost a lot of time killing flies. If I didn't watch out the summer would be gone and I wouldn't be ready for Mr. Stern's test.

Beginning on Monday, Ed watched the mailbox eagerly for a letter telling him that he'd won the fly-swatting contest. Day after day nothing came. Except rain. Lots of rain.

"Looks like the drought that drove the homesteaders away in 1909 and 1910 is finally over," Papa said.

"Thank goodness!" Mama exclaimed.

"I bet the rain hasn't helped the Chamber of Commerce with the fly-counting business," Papa observed.

"Yeah," Ed agreed, brightening up a bit. "That's prob'ly why I haven't heard anything yet."

"Probably is," Papa echoed. I could imagine what a mess our manure-filled sacks would be now that they were soaking wet. Other than that, I appreciated the rainy weather. It gave me more time to read. I was nearly finished with the first book.

Ed thumbed through the Sears Roebuck catalog, trying to decide what he'd buy with his money. "I can get a jackknife for forty-five cents," he said, "plus five cents postage. Or a thumb-trigger rifle for two twenty-five. But the Quackenbush Junior Safety Rifle is better. It costs three dollars and ninety-five cents, plus bullets, of course."

"How much are the bullets?" Frank asked, looking over Ed's shoulder.

"Fifty for fourteen cents," Ed said, and turned some more pages. "This J. B. Stetson sombrero is three dollars, and a Texas Chief Cowboy Hat costs five twenty-five."

"How much postage?" Frank asked.

"Thirty-eight cents."

"We could get a new saddle for three dollars and eighty cents, or . . ."

"An all-steel wood-beam one-horse plow for two twelve," Papa said from across the room. "That's what I need. And a single-breast collar buggy harness for four ninety-five." Ed wasn't the only one who'd studied the catalog.

"How about a bathtub for twenty-seven dollars and fifteen cents?" Mama asked in her you-might-just-as-well-wish-for-the-moon voice.

"How about indoor plumbing first?" Papa teased. "A bathtub with two holes in the top and one in the bottom wouldn't be much good without pipes to fill and drain it."

I was working on a quilt block with a flyswatter and lots of flies buzzing around on a square that was as orange as the hot summer sun. Just as I threaded the needle with black to make lazy-daisy stitches for the wings, someone knocked on the door. Mama answered.

"It's for you, Dora."

There stood Mrs. Tracy, tears shining in her eyes.

"Where's Jimmie Joe?" I asked.

"I left him with Peter Paul," she said. "He's awfully good with his baby brother."

I invited Mrs. Tracy into the front room, and Mama brought her a glass of water.

"I've finally been going through Cora Beth's things," Mrs. Tracy said, "and I know that she'd want you to have this." It was my friend's dictionary. Mrs. Tracy couldn't say anything else and neither could I. We just hugged each other for a while and cried.

I told her how much I needed that book this summer and how I would keep it all my life and think of Cora Beth every time I used it. "I'm glad," she said, smiling sadly.

As she stood to leave she said, "You haven't been to visit us for a long time. You need to come over and see how big Jimmie Joe is. He's crawling everywhere now."

"I will," I promised. Yes, I'd probably be able to do it after this much time.

"You're the only daughter I have left," she choked, giving me another hard hug before she hurried away.

The very next day Ed got a letter inviting him to come in to the Chamber of Commerce office. The letter didn't say if he was the winner of the first prize or the forty-first, or even if he was a winner at all.

"They wouldn't bother to write you," Papa reasoned, "if you hadn't won something. Let's all put on our best clothes and ride over to Clovis to find out what's what."

On the way, we talked about the possibilities.

"You'll be rich if you win!" Caroline said. "Seventeen dollars and fifty cents is a lot of money."

"You mean *we'll* be rich," Ed corrected her. "Everyone helped, and everyone gets part of the money."

"You and Dora did most of the work," Frank acknowledged.

"Everyone did as much as they could," Ed insisted. "I'll divide it nine ways."

It didn't take me long to figure out that that meant one dollar and ninety-four cents for each person. That was a lot less than seventeen fifty. But it was a lot *more* than any of us had ever had before—except Papa, of course.

Ed wasn't as good as I was with arithmetic, and I was sure he hadn't figured out how much he'd get in the end. I decided not to tell him. He'd know soon enough.

"Well," Caroline reminded him, "you'd better *get* the money before you give it all away."

Papa sent Ed into the Chamber of Commerce office by himself while everyone else waited in the wagon. He came out waving an envelope with his name on it. "First prize!" he shouted to the family, and pulled out a check signed by B. D. Oldham. He passed the important piece of paper around so everyone could look at it.

"How can I divide this?" Ed wondered.

"Cash it," Papa said, and drove us over to the Clovis National Bank. He went inside with Ed, and when they came out, Ed was jangling coins in both pockets. Everyone jumped down out of the wagon to see.

"Line up," Ed instructed, "and hold out a hand." He placed a silver dollar in each outstretched palm and saved one for himself. Mama wanted to hold the baby's money for her, but Irene clutched it fiercely and wouldn't let go.

Ed counted how many dollars he had left. There were only eight. He turned to me with his what-do-I-do-now look. "Trade them for halves," I whispered.

Ed went back inside the bank to do that, and after each person got a half dollar, he exchanged what was left for quarters. He passed those around, too. Then he traded the rest of the quarters for dimes, the remaining dimes for nickels, and finally he had only a handful of pennies. He gave out nine of those.

"Now," he said, "you each have one silver dollar, one fifty-cent piece, one quarter, one dime, one nickel, and one penny, and"—he hesitated to count the coins he had left—"there's thirty-one cents to spend."

"For what?" Caroline wanted to know.

"Candy, to begin with," Ed told us. "Everyone can pick out his favorite kind."

We all trooped into Vanderwart's General Mercantile, next door. While everyone else debated over which variety of penny candy to choose, I watched Ed. He picked up a jackknife to see how it felt in his hand, asked the price, and laid it down again. He rubbed his fingers over the soft felt of a cowboy hat and bounced a rubber ball on the floor. Finally he settled for a pretty twenty-cent sugar bowl. He paid for that and nine cents for the candy.

"I don't need a sugar bowl," Mama whispered, thinking Ed had bought it for her.

"I do," Ed said.

"What for?" Papa asked.

"To keep my money in," Ed said, and dropped the extra two cents inside. Then he pulled his other coins from his pocket and put them in, too.

"Will you keep mine?" I asked, holding out my fistful of money. He nodded and I dropped it in.

"Mine?" Howard added his.

"Mine!" Irene shouted.

"Pooh," Caroline said, putting her hand behind her back. "I'm keeping my own."

"Me too," Frank insisted, reaching into his pocket to make sure the money was still there. George was trying to decide what to do about his share.

"Can I get it out anytime I want it?" he asked.

"Of course," Ed assured him. "Anytime."

George added his cash to the sugar bowl, and so did Papa and Mama. Ed looked at the accumulating pile and grinned. "Maybe we can buy something for the whole family," he suggested, "when we decide what we want."

"Good idea," Papa said, and Mama nodded.

When we got home, Ed counted out the money into individual piles again and tied each person's share of the prize in a different-colored scrap of cloth. Then he put the wrapped packages back in his bank and set it on top of the kitchen cupboard.

Occasionally, someone asked for one of his own coins to spend. Sometimes, on Sunday afternoon, we'd get out the Sears Roebuck catalog and look through it to see what we wanted. Matching cowboy sombreros? We found some "heavyweight wool" ones for $1.50 each. A new saddle? A horse blanket?

Every once in a while we'd decide on something and Ed would get his bank down and count out the right amount of money.

"But if we just had fifty cents more," he'd say, "we could get something better." So we'd decide to save our pennies until we had enough. The problem was that pennies were hard to come by, and it took a long, long time for us to accumulate fifty more. By then, our desires had changed and Ed would say, "But if we just had twenty-five cents more, we could get a bigger or better one."

We always needed just a little more money than we

had. It got so that every time Ed took down the sugar bowl one of us would tease, "It's no use. There won't be enough money."

We started saying, "Get out the if-we-just-had-a-little-more-money book" when we meant the catalog. Finally I figured out that *having* money was more important to Ed than spending it. He'd figured out the perfect way to make sure nothing happened to our hard-earned coins.

Frank was different from Ed. He thought he needed to *spend* money to *make* money. He had decided how he'd do it.

"I'm going to buy fifteen Silver Spangler Hamburg eggs for a dollar and fifty cents," he said, "and raise chickens. I'll sell those to buy a porker to fatten. Then I'll sell that and buy a lamb. After that I'll get a calf and, finally, a colt so I'll have my own horse." While everyone else's money sat in the bank, Frank kept his working for him.

I made a quilt block showing Ed's sugar bowl bank and finished *Fairy Tales.* After the fly-swatting contest, I needed to catch up with my reading schedule. When I opened *The Children's Own Longfellow,* Miss Foster's note instructed me to "choose one to memorize."

The rainy weather gave me time to read but put us way behind on the summer work. The garden was growing like crazy.

"Those free seeds you ordered from the government," Papa told Mama, "are sure the best varieties available. I've never seen anything like the way they're producing. You'll be hard put to get everything taken care of before it gets too old."

"I'll have to have a lot of help," Mama said.

That meant us. It was time for the summer canning to begin.

17

Downhill Toward Fall

The rest of the summer was a blur. I couldn't figure out why Papa called it "canning" when we never filled cans, only jars. We filled jar after jar after jar. Beets, beans, and chard; pickles, piccalilli, and relish; tomatoes, tomato juice, chili sauce, and catsup; jellies, jams, preserves, and marmalade; apricots, plums, peaches, pears, and apples—two or three batches a day. The basement shelves glowed with all kinds and colors of bottled fruit and vegetables. Mama proudly called them her *jewels*. "That's my money in the bank," she said. I decided my next quilt block would have jars in all colors sitting on the cellar shelves.

I had to do my reading in short snatches of time whenever there was a break in the summer jobs. Longfellow's poems were harder to read than the fairy tales had been, but there were only eight of them. I had to look up a lot of the words. Thank goodness for Cora Beth's dictionary.

I'd been too busy with other things to spend much time moping about the loss of my friend, but every once in a while something would trigger a memory that left an empty ache in the pit of my stomach. Using her dictionary did that. But even though I felt sad, I was happy to have such a precious reminder of our time together. I'd made up my mind that I'd never let myself have such a close friend again. It hurt too much when she was gone. I was nearly ready to visit the Tracys once more but never found the right time to do it.

Hiawatha's Fishing was the Longfellow poem I chose to memorize. It told how an Indian boy went out in his canoe determined to catch the biggest fish in the stream—the sturgeon, king of fishes. He would not be content with anything else. This made the sturgeon angry:

From the white sand of the bottom
Up he rose with angry gesture,
Quivering in each nerve and fibre,
Clashing all his plates of armor,
Gleaming bright with all his warpaint;
In his wrath he darted upward,

Flashing leaped into the sunshine,
Opened his great jaws, and swallowed
Both canoe and Hiawatha.

The rest of the poem told how the boy was rescued from the belly of the sturgeon by his animal friends. The tale was a good one to recite.

I finally finished *The Children's Own Longfellow* and eagerly opened the next book. Miss Foster's note had only one word on it: "Enjoy." That proved to be the understatement of the summer.

I fell in love with spunky, redheaded Anne of Green Gables at once. She was a bright, fun-loving girl who couldn't seem to stay out of trouble. She was always talking about the scope of her imagination. There was no explanation of why Miss Foster thought I should read that book, but I decided it must have something to do with all the big words.

Would Mr. Stern expect me to spell words like *embowered, enraptured, presumptuous, unaccountably, predilection,* or *amethyst*? Would he ask me what they meant? Just in case, I wrote them down and looked them up in the dictionary—*my* dictionary now.

Pretty soon I got too interested in what was happening in the book to care about the reason for reading it. I'd think about that later. Besides all the wonderful adventures, I loved the way Anne painted pictures with words. When she told about beautiful Avonlea on Prince Edward Island, I felt like I was back in Utah again. I remembered my own Lake of Shining Waters—Silver Lake at Brighton, up Big Cottonwood Canyon. In springtime I, too, had walked through a Great White Way of apple blossoms down the lane to Grandma's. Would our puny New Mexico orchard ever be as beautiful?

I knew exactly what the Snow Queen cherry tree looked like from a second-story window because Aunt Isabel had one just like it outside her bedroom. And a purple Violet Vale below. When Anne described Diana Barry's garden, it seemed like I was home again greeting the same flowers by their names—peony, bleeding heart, narcissus, and columbine.

I remembered the huge rugged mountains and the foothills that blazed with the fire of red maples in the fall. Would I ever see a mountain again? Or red maples? Would I ever get used to this rusty, flat land with no mountains, no canyons, and no trees? Even the sand hills were so low that they were almost invisible until you were in them. Would New Mexico ever seem as beautiful to me as Utah?

Summer was coasting downhill toward fall, and I was thinking that if I were in charge of the calendar, New Year's Day would be in the fall. That's the time of year when everything finished and started up again.

The crops were harvested, the trees dropped their leaves, the flowers froze, and life on the farm wound down.

In the fall, school began again and everyone moved up a grade. It was time for handed-down clothes, new books, and exciting hopes and dreams. That's when New Year's should be. Not in the middle of the winter, at the beginning of January, the dullest month of all.

Autumn was the time of year we'd waved good-bye to Utah and said hello to New Mexico, the time we'd filed our claim for the homestead farm. Even my birthday was at the end of summer. Maybe that's the reason I thought the new year should begin then—because my own always did.

I finished the yellow quilt square with Mama's jars of jewels. Only two more blocks to do and I'd have twelve—another place to stop and begin again. I'd make a dozen more next year and then decide what to do about the extra twenty-four squares I'd have left because of the change in the homestead law. I wanted to stitch the blocks together using Mama's machine but wasn't sure yet how they'd be arranged.

I laid them out on Mama's bed in rainbow stripes—two of each color. Each one made me think of something special. The kangaroo rat in Miss Foster's desk, stitched on a red square, started me giggling again. Mama's sewing machine on an orange block came next, then a yellow square showing off her bottled fruit, then Henrietta's tombstone in a grassy field, and after that, the blue block showing the heart-shaped wreath on Cora Beth's grave. Frank's kachina mask, on purple, finished the first row. I arranged the second row with the New Mexico map, a flyswatter with flies, Ed's sugar bowl bank, and the pink pork carcass hanging from a hoist. The second green block was still blank, and so was the blue one. I was saving one to write "FIFTH GRADE" on if I passed Mr. Stern's test. There was still time to figure out the other one before Homestead Day. The squares were not in the same order the events happened. I hadn't thought about that when I'd chosen the colors.

The canning was not quite finished when it was time to start getting ready for school to begin.

First, we had to try on shoes so we could order the new ones we needed from the Sears Roebuck catalog soon enough. We lined up in a row on the back porch, and Mama got out the box she'd put away when school was out. Our bare feet had all grown during the summer so no one could wear the same pair as last year.

"Pass them on down," Mama instructed.

Caroline handed hers to me, Ed gave his to Frank, Frank pushed his to George, and George passed his to Howard.

"Now try them on," Mama said.

"These're too tight for me," I complained.

Mama felt them to see.

"No, they're not," she insisted. "It's just that you aren't used to wearing shoes."

"How come Caroline always gets the new ones?" I grumbled.

"And Ed," Frank said.

"Because they're the biggest," Mama explained.

"That's not fair!" I objected.

"No one ever said that life was fair," Mama said impatiently. "Maybe you can tell me what Ed and Caroline will wear for shoes if they don't get some new ones. You know very well that there are none to hand down to them."

Even though we were supposed to be up and over the top of the rainbow, going downhill didn't seem any easier than climbing up had. The broomcorn crop was abundant because of all the rain, but Papa hadn't been paid for it yet. And when he was, most of the money would be spent to buy what we needed for the farm. Extra pennies were scarce. We still had most of our swat-the-fly-contest cash in Ed's bank, and he was still making sure we didn't spend it.

"I never get anything new," I grumbled.

"Have you already forgotten last year?" Mama asked gently. "You had a new dress *and* new shoes to start school, remember?" Was that only last year? It seemed a century ago. Mama hugged me to show there were no hard feelings over our argument.

While we waited for the new shoes to come, Mama put patches on the boys' overalls and let down the hems of last year's dresses. "There's simply no money to buy new ones," she said. "But I'll make them so pretty no one will ever notice. Bring me the bias tape, Dora. I'll cover up the old fold marks and stitch on a new trim at the same time. Get the blue for Caroline's dress and the pink for yours."

"Have you finished all your reading yet?" she asked when I returned with the tape.

"I'm nearly done," I told her.

When I got to the part in the book where Anne was studying for the entrance examination to Queen's Academy, it was like me getting ready for Mr. Stern's test into fifth grade—except that by then Anne was not a child any longer but a young lady. Girls surely grew up a lot faster in books than in real life.

As I turned the last page, I felt sad I'd come to the end. I wanted to keep on reading. For ever and ever. I had never enjoyed any book more than *Anne of Green Gables.*

As I sat thinking, not ready yet to close the book, I noticed Miss Foster's folded note. I opened the page and read:

Dear Dora,

I hope you had a pleasant time perusing these books. The fairy tales and Longfellow were intended to enrich your experience with fourth-reader authors, but Anne of Green Gables *was meant purely for pleasure. With her active imagination and determination to do things, she reminds me a great deal of you, though, thank goodness, you lack her propensity for getting into trouble.*

It might be a good idea to review some of the fourth grade arithmetic papers and go over your notes about New Mexico. Take a good look at the state map, too. History and geography are very important to Mr. Stern.

Your test is scheduled for 9:00 A.M. on August 29 at the schoolhouse. With a memory like yours, I'm sure you will do fine. Don't forget that I will be back from summer vacation, and while you take the test I will be right next door getting my room ready to start school. I'll be thinking about you and silently cheering you on.

When you move into fifth grade (I'm confident you will), I hope you will continue to develop your skills as an elocutionist. That talent can bring much pleasure to others as well as to yourself. I've never had such an eager student as you and probably never will again. I will miss having you in my room.

Sincerely,

Miss Letitia Foster

Oh, Miss Foster, I thought, *how I will miss* you—*your love of learning, your Cleopatra voice, your stranger-than-fiction stories. Even your underlined words intended to increase my vocabulary.*

Letitia. What a lovely name. It sounded like poetry and must mean something wonderful and bright. Something beautiful. Letitia. I stored it in my brain to suggest for the baby when it came time for *L* in our alphabetical family—provided the tenth child was a girl, of course.

I wondered if either Miss Foster or Mr. Stern knew that the test was scheduled on my eleventh birthday. I decided it would be a present to myself if I passed that test! I pulled the sheaf of papers from my chest to study.

All the members of my family helped me get ready. Mama, Papa, Caroline, Ed, and Frank took turns asking me questions about the information on the sheets. George and Howard did my job of bringing the cow home from the pasture so I'd have more time to study. Irene listened to the poems I'd memorized.

The day of the test, I realized most of that reviewing wasn't necessary. Living, not studying, had prepared me for the examination.

All the arithmetic problems were adding, subtracting, dividing, and multiplying three- or four-digit numbers—exactly the kind I'd had plenty of practice with while we were counting dead flies. I knew how many teaspoons in a tablespoon, tablespoons in a cup, cups in a quart, quarts in a gallon, and pecks in a bushel. I'd been measuring them out all summer while we bottled fruit. I remembered the kachinas from the boys' mask and exactly how to make Pueblo pueblos, Apache dresses, and cradle boards. I knew the length of the Santa Fe Trail because I'd compared the mileage to our own trip from Utah. I could answer all the questions about the Turquoise Trail. Hadn't I pretended to walk along it to trade sky-blue stones for parrot feathers and abalone shells in Mexico?

I knew about the Spanish conquerors, too. I'd never forget Miss Foster's story of Coronado's expedition hunting for the seven golden Cities of Cíbola, how the explorers traveled from February to July, finally found a few adobe houses, and then stopped, wanting water more than gold. It was easy to figure out the date New Mexico became a state because I remembered that it happened the first Saturday in 1912 and New Year's Day was the Monday before. I knew how many stars the new flag had: forty-eight—the same number as my quilt blocks.

I could name the principal rivers and most of the counties in New Mexico. After struggling as long as I did to make that map, they were permanently impressed on my brain.

When Mr. Stern said my time was up, I looked at the clock. I couldn't believe I'd been writing for two hours.

After the test was over, I went into the room next door to talk to Miss Foster. She looked down from the ladder she was standing on to tack some pictures to the wall and said, "Happy Birthday, Dora." Of course, Miss Foster would remember! I could tell by the way she smiled that she was sure I'd passed the test. The idea went through my head that maybe she'd volunteered to *write* the examination for Mr. Stern. That's exactly the kind of thing she'd do. Oh, how I loved my teacher!

Suddenly, I realized what I had done. In my rush to catch up to my class, I had hurried right through the best year of my life and had left the most wonderful teacher in the world behind. I had passed up the chance to be in her room for three more years. On the other hand, thanks to Miss Foster's help, I'd finished *four* grades in *one* year. We'd had lots of pleasant, private time together. I couldn't ask for more than that.

I helped Miss Foster put new alphabet cards around

the room while I waited for Mr. Stern to correct the test and tell me the results. Finally he opened the door, poked his head in, and nodded. That was all.

Miss Foster grabbed me in a hug and whispered, with tears in her eyes, "I knew you could do it!"

"Thanks to you!" I said, squeezing her around the waist. I handed her the report card with the question mark on it. She filled in the blank so it said: "Promoted to Grade 5." Then she gave me a loving pat on my behind and said, "Now run along home and celebrate with your family."

So I did.

Everyone was in the kitchen waiting for me. The table was set for dinner with an eleven-candle birthday cake in the center. When I told them the good news, Papa stood up and lifted his hand in the air. "Let's hear eleven hurrahs for Dora before we sit down to eat," he said.

After we finished the cake and cleared the table, Mama brought a big box in from the porch.

"What's that?" I asked.

"Don't know," she said.

"Probably a birthday present," Papa said. "It has your name on it."

"Where did it come from?" I wanted to know.

Caroline read the return address. "Utah," she said. "Holladay, Utah. Someone named Cookson," she added with a tease in her voice.

"Grandma?" I asked.

"Or one of the aunts?" Mama said. "We have lots of Cookson relatives in Holladay, Utah."

"Well open it, for Pete's sake, and let's find out," Ed said.

"It might be some of Cousin Mandy's outgrown clothes for Mama to make over," I guessed, clipping the twine, tearing off the paper, and opening the box. On top of a pile of clothes lay a tissue-wrapped object. As soon as I picked it up, I could tell it was a doll.

It must have been a hand-me-down from Mandy, but it looked brand-new. It was beautiful, with real hair and blue eyes that opened and closed, just like Cora Beth's doll, Rose Marie. The dress was pink organdy with lace ruffles around the bottom. Blue ribbons were tied in bows to hang down from the yoke.

It seemed to me that the angels in heaven, maybe even Cora Beth herself, must have made that beautiful doll. I named her Angela, for the angels, and planned to use my blue quilt block to picture her sitting on a white cloud like she was floating down from heaven.

"Did you write to Aunt Zoe and tell her what happened to Henrietta?" I asked Mama suspiciously.

"I could have mentioned it," Mama said. "I write so many letters, I can't remember everything I say in them."

So God had used Mama, Cousin Mandy, and Aunt Zoe. And he had waited for me to decide I could get along without a doll before he answered my prayer.

"Angela's too pretty to play with," I said, hugging her close. "I'll keep her where I can look at her every day and save her for Irene when she's older."

August 29 had already been an eventful day, but I needed to do one more thing.

Catching up to my class had been Cora Beth's idea. I wanted to share the news with her family that I had done it. On the way, I stopped at the cemetery. I figured my friend was probably looking down from heaven when I tucked my report card between the grass and the grave marker. I made sure "Promoted to Grade 5" was showing so she could read it.

I felt strange knocking on the Tracys' door when I used to walk right in, but it seemed like the polite thing to do when I'd been away so long. As soon as Mrs. Tracy saw me, she grabbed me in a hug that almost squeezed my breath away. Jimmie Joe peeked out from behind his papa's legs. He didn't even remember me. When I blurted out my news, Sam Houston and Robert Lee both said, "We'll be in the same room!" They sounded happy about it. A framed picture on the piano was the only sign of Cora Beth, but every corner of the house was familiar to me, and I still felt at home there. I started to sing one of the songs I used to croon to Jimmie Joe and held out my arms to him. I didn't leave until we were friends again.

Later that night, as I climbed the ladder to my bed in the loft, I thought about being in fifth grade. I remembered one of Mama's repeated warnings: "Be careful what you wish for; you might be disappointed when you get it."

Would I *really* be glad to be in Mr. Stern's room? Could I cope with the cracker?

The doubt only lasted for a moment. With a family like mine, the support of the Tracys, and Miss Foster in the room next door, how could I possibly fail?